MW01017329

HALEY
and The Big BLAST

A.E. Scotland

Amy Elise Press

SEATTLE, WA

*This book is dedicated to girls
who have a love of science,
the desire to learn,
and a generous heart.*

ISBN 0-9776760-2-1
Library of Congress Control Number: 2005939127

Amy Elise Press
An Imprint of **Foundations for Girls, Inc.**
Seattle, WA

For more information visit:
www.AmyElise.com
www.FoundationsForGirls.com

Book Design: Molly Murrah, Murrah & Company, Kirkland, WA

CONTENTS

～ CHAPTER 1 ～

Dead Fish Don't Eat Cheese Puffs

Haley Bellamy was a scientist.

She knew some people might think a 10-year old girl too young to be a scientist, but Haley firmly believed she was one, and more. In fact, she saw herself as both a scientist and an inventor. She was forever trying to solve problems using her knowledge of scientific facts and theories, or building contraptions from things she found around her house.

It was natural Haley would think of herself as a scientist since she came from a long line of scientific Bellamys. Her great-grandfather was John R. Bellamy, famous for inventing Bellamy Drift, which was a navigation method he developed for World War II fighter and bomber aircraft. Her grandfather was John R. Bellamy Jr., widely known for his work in chemistry. Haley's aunt, Gabrielle Bellamy, was a renowned physicist in the area of lasers and optics.

The family science genes seemed to have skipped her father, John R. Bellamy III. He was a quality assurance supervisor in an automotive manufacturing plant and seemed to have little interest in science. Fortunately, however, most of her father's missing science genes landed squarely in Haley.

Given her family's long lineage of esteemed scientists, Haley was certain she would have been named John R. Bellamy IV, except for two important facts. First, she was a girl. The name *John* would be a strange name for a girl. Second, her parents had the poor judgment to have another baby before they had her.

The other baby was her older brother. He had arrived four years before Haley and, accordingly, received the title John R. Bellamy IV. Everyone called him "J.R." to avoid confusion with her father. Now he was 14 years old, and the closest thing to being a scientist he displayed was riding around on his skateboard.

Haley did not mind that her name was not John. Obviously, a girl named John would be ridiculous. Besides, she liked her name better. Her father often joked that she was named after Haley's comet. "My girl of sparks and shooting stars," he would say when arriving home from work and scooping Haley up in his arms.

At the moment, Haley was carefully scanning the contents of the refrigerator. She was not conducting an experiment; rather, she was on a more important mission—finding a snack. She studied each shelf. The apples looked soft in places. She was not in the mood for an orange. Yogurt was too healthy. Cheese was a possibility. Sliced pepperoni sounded better. Her concentration was shattered by her mother's voice.

"Haley," Mrs. Bellamy called from across the family room, where she was sitting at the table doing paperwork. "You've had that refrigerator door open long enough. You're letting all the cold air out. It costs more money when the refrigerator has to work harder. Close the door until you figure out what you want."

Today was Monday. Mrs. Bellamy worked as a part-time accountant Monday through Thursday. She worked in her office while Haley was in school and from home in the afternoons. She often described things in terms of how much they cost.

Curled next to Mrs. Bellamy's feet was the family dog, Einstein. Einstein was a beagle and had been a gift from Haley's scientist aunt. Einstein was old now and quite fat. His once brown face was mostly gray. These days, he slept, searched for handouts, and occasionally barked when someone knocked at the front door.

Haley closed the refrigerator door. She turned, furrowed her eyebrows, and frowned at her mother. Mrs. Bellamy did not notice. She had already turned her attention back to her accounting paperwork. Haley sighed. What was the point of frowning if no one notices, she thought.

She turned her attention back to her snack-finding mission. Haley stuck her head through the pantry door and started to rummage among the boxes of cereal and bags of snack foods. This was her lucky day! She found a newly opened bag of Cheese Puffs. She knew she had better get some now before her brother came home. If he found the Cheese Puffs, the bag would magically disappear into his room and Haley would not get any.

Her mother called out again. "Haley," she said, "would you mind taking the garbage can to the street? Tomorrow is trash day."

Haley backed out of the pantry, held the Cheese Puffs up with one hand toward her mother, and pointed to the bag with the other. She scrunched her face into a distressed look and tried a whiny voice. "But Mom, I'm really hungry now. Can't I take the garbage out after I eat?" she said.

Mrs. Bellamy did not look up from her papers. "Just take the garbage out, honey. You can have your snack right after."

Haley could tell she was fully absorbed in her work. She was always mystified why her mother found accounting so riveting while expressing utter puzzlement at Haley's infatuation with science. Her mother never discouraged Haley from science, she just simply did not understand Haley's interest.

Haley knew whenever her mother was busy with work, it was best to do as she asked. Although her mother would have no reaction to good things going on around her as she worked, she somehow managed to notice trouble immediately. It was as though Mrs. Bellamy had a "trouble antenna" attached to her head, always scanning for signs. Haley wondered if it were possible to surgically implant a metal antenna into a person's head and wire it to her brain.

Haley lowered her hand holding the Cheese Puffs and let the bag dangle at her side. She did not want her brother to come home and find the Cheese Puffs while she took out the garbage. Haley thought hard and looked around the kitchen for a good Cheese Puffs hiding spot. Her razor-sharp blue eyes lit upon a portable ice chest nestled under the overhang of the kitchen counter.

Mr. Bellamy, Haley's father, had used the ice chest over the weekend during a fishing trip. Haley lifted the lid and peered inside. Two large fish rested upon dry ice wrapped in thick brown paper. Mr. Bellamy liked using dry ice instead of regular ice. Haley knew it was colder than regular ice and did not melt the same way. Regular ice would melt into water first and then turn into a gas as the water evaporated. Dry ice skipped the melting part. It simply evaporated directly. The fish peered back at her with lifeless eyes.

The ice chest was a perfect hiding place. J.R. would never think to look there, even if he knew about the Cheese Puffs. Haley quickly placed the bag in the ice chest and closed the top. She grabbed the plastic bag of garbage from the kitchen trash can.

The laundry room led to the garage and was the fastest route. She went that way. The garage door was open. She made her way through

it, trying not to knock over the bicycles or bump against her mother's minivan. Her brother's skateboard was in the way, as it always was. She stepped over it.

The garbage can was in a corner just inside the garage. It was made of metal, with a rimmed bottom that made it hard to drag over any surface. Haley lifted the lid and dropped the kitchen bag into the can.

The garbage can was not too full, but it was still heavy. Haley tugged at the can. It moved a little. She tugged harder and dragged it across the smooth surface of the garage floor to the start of the driveway. At the edge, Haley's driveway angled steeply downward to the sidewalk and street. The driveway looked like it was made of gravel placed into concrete, creating a rough surface. Despite the steep slope, the garbage can moved slowly, resisting Haley's efforts.

"There's gotta be an easier way," Haley grumbled to herself. "Why didn't they just make the driveway smooth? I bet there'd be less friction with a smooth surface." She pulled the garbage can halfway down the driveway, and stopped to take a breather.

At the sound of squeaky bicycle brakes, Haley looked up. A girl straddled a bike at the end of the driveway, watching Haley. The girl appeared to be about the same age and height as Haley, but she had flaming red hair that was swept back and looked like it was permanently wind-blown. Her flaming hair matched the fiery brown eyes set behind shiny gold-rimmed glasses. A mass of freckles covered her nose and spread equally across her cheeks.

"What'cha doing Haley?" asked the red-haired girl.

"Hey Red!" Haley said brightly.

Red's real name was Meredith Elise Sheridan. She was Haley's best friend. No one, including Haley, ever called her by her given name. Everyone simply called her Red. Even her parents called her Red, unless she was in trouble.

"I'm taking out the garbage. It's my month," Haley said, shrugging her shoulders. Haley and J.R. alternated months for certain household jobs. "The can's kinda heavy this time. Can you give me a hand?"

"Sure," replied Red. She dismounted from her bike.

Red pushed while Haley pulled. With the two of them, the garbage can slid more easily, although occasionally it still got stuck. They pushed and pulled the can until it sat at the edge of the street.

"Thanks for your help," Haley said. "The trash is too heavy and the driveway is too rough to do it by myself easily."

"Maybe you can come up with some way to make it slide more easily, or come up with some other contraption," Red suggested. "You could ask your aunt for ideas the next time she comes over."

Gabrielle Bellamy, Haley's scientist aunt, visited frequently, usually weekly. Haley rubbed her chin. She had the habit of rubbing her chin when she started to think about solving problems. "Aunt Gabby's coming over tomorrow night. Maybe I'll ask her then," she said thoughtfully.

Haley's stomach rumbled. She realized she still had not eaten her snack. "Red, do you want to come inside for a snack? I found some Cheese Puffs. I had to hide them with some dead fish in my Dad's ice cooler so J.R. won't find them. I'm pretty sure the fish won't eat them," she said, looking sideways at Red.

"You hid your Cheese Puffs with dead fish!" exclaimed Red. She wrinkled her nose. "Won't they taste fishy from the fish smell?"

"No. I don't think so," Haley said. "The fish didn't smell fishy in the ice cooler." She grinned. "Besides, better fishy Cheese Puffs than no Cheese Puffs."

"Nah, I'll pass." Red sounded skeptical. "Anyway, I'm on my way to my piano lesson. I gotta get going." She mounted her bicycle and rode off again down the street.

Haley watched her go. Talking about Cheese Puffs made her even hungrier. She headed back inside.

⌐ CHAPTER 2 ⌐

The Problem With Root Beer

Haley went back through the garage and inside her house to the kitchen. Mrs. Bellamy was still working at the family table. Haley opened the lid to the portable cooler. The bag of Cheese Puffs was still safely nestled against the dead fish. She grabbed the bag and put it on the counter. A vision of pepperoni slices flashed in her mind. She opened the refrigerator, fetched the pepperoni slices, and placed them next to the Cheese Puffs. Haley made one last scan of the refrigerator. Her eyes lit upon a two-liter plastic bottle of root beer. She grabbed it before she closed the refrigerator door.

She carefully arranged Cheese Puffs and pepperoni slices on a plate, poured herself a cup of root beer, and carried both over to the family table. As Haley sat, Mrs. Bellamy glanced over.

"What! Cheese Puffs! Pepperoni! Soda!" Mrs. Bellamy looked mortified. "What kind of snack is that?" she demanded.

Haley scrunched down in her chair and clasped her hands together in her lap. She raised her eyebrows and put on her best innocent smile. "I took out the garbage just like you asked. I already got out the food. Please?" she pleaded.

Mrs. Bellamy looked exasperated. "All right," she sighed. "I just hope other people don't see this. They'll think I'm a bad mother." She again turned her attention to her paperwork.

Relieved, Haley started munching on Cheese Puffs. Soon her fingers turned yellowish-orange. She reached into her back pocket and pulled out her ever-present magnifying glass. It had been a gift from her grandfather, John R. Bellamy Jr. The handle and rim were brass, which gave it a nice heft. An inscription was engraved along the length of the handle. *To Haley, Love Grandpa* it read. Whether Haley wore school clothes, pants, or a Sunday dress, she always kept the magnifying glass with her.

She rotated her hand slowly and studied her fingers carefully under the magnifying glass. Satisfied, she put it on the table and picked up two slices of pepperoni, one in each hand. She tilted her chin up. With one hand she dangled a piece of pepperoni just above her mouth. Haley snapped at it several times and clicked her teeth as though she were a shark snapping at a small fish. While she was doing that, she discreetly placed her other hand holding the second pepperoni slice underneath the table. She heard Einstein rustle as he noticed the morsel in her hand. She felt his wet nose as he carefully took the pepperoni slice. A minute later, she felt him come back and start licking her Cheese Puff covered fingers. Then Haley took her cup of root beer and filled her cheeks with soda, wanting to savor the taste.

Splat!

Haley spit the root beer out of her mouth and all over the table, including on Mrs. Bellamy's paperwork. The root beer was flat!

"Ack!" Mrs. Bellamy cried. "What're you doing, Haley! You got soda all over my work."

Einstein scampered out from underneath the table and looked around. Haley felt guilty. "The soda was flat. There wasn't any fizz in it at all. It tasted terrible!" She tried to use her sleeve to mop up the root beer on the table.

"No, no, no. Don't wipe it with your sleeve. Go get a towel or sponge or something," said Mrs. Bellamy.

Haley jumped up, grabbed a towel from the kitchen, and raced back to the table. Mrs. Bellamy tried to use the towel to dry her papers. It was not working well. She gathered them in a rough pile. "I'm going to take my papers upstairs and lay them out to dry. While I'm doing that, you need to clean up this mess," said Mrs. Bellamy.

"Don't worry Mom, I'll clean it up and throw away the rest of the soda," Haley said.

Mrs. Bellamy shook her head. "Don't throw away the soda. It costs money and there's no sense wasting it. Someone will drink it later," she added, as she left the room.

The towel remained on the table in a sad damp pile. Haley tucked her magnifying glass in her pocket, cleared the rest of the table, and used the sponge to scrub the sticky spots. She put the pepperoni and soda away in the refrigerator. The Cheese Puff bag was still on the counter. She did not want J.R. to eat the rest. She looked around. Only Einstein was watching, and she knew he would never tell anyone. Haley opened the cooler and carefully placed the Cheese Puff bag next to the dead fish. She stared at the brown wrapping paper holding the dry ice.

"Hmm," she murmured. An idea started to form as her mind churned. Absentmindedly, she rubbed her chin.

From underneath the fish, she lifted the brown packaging and placed it on the counter. She opened the refrigerator, pulled the root beer from the shelf, and placed it on the counter next to the brown paper.

Her mind began to work harder and harder. She pressed her nose against the soda bottle. What makes the fizz in soda? She knew it was carbon dioxide, an odorless and colorless gas. Haley turned to the brown wrapping paper.

Carefully, she opened the paper until the block of ice was visible. She remembered that dry ice was nothing more than frozen carbon dioxide. Using her magnifying glass, she peered closely at it. Small wisps were coming off the surface. Before her eyes, she could see the dry ice converting directly to carbon dioxide gas.

Haley was excited. If dry ice was carbon dioxide, and it went directly to a gas when melted, then maybe dry ice could put the fizz back into the soda bottle! She could not wait to try her experiment to see if it worked.

She knew she had to be careful. Her father often warned her to avoid touching dry ice directly because it was so cold it could actually burn the skin if accidentally touched. Avoiding a burn was her first problem. Her second problem was how to get the dry ice into the soda bottle. The opening was small, so only tiny pieces of ice would fit.

Haley looked in the kitchen drawers for something that might be helpful. She found a meat tenderizing hammer and gently tapped on a corner of the dry ice until she had a number of small pieces. Next, she took scissors, cut a piece from the wrapping paper, and curved the paper into the shape of a funnel. Haley inserted the small end of the funnel into the bottle opening and held it so she could brush pieces of dry ice into the top of the funnel.

Using a pencil from the pencil jar, she brushed in several pieces and watched them slide down the funnel and disappear into the bottle. She kept brushing in ice until she ran out of pieces, then placed the bottle on the counter.

Numerous bits of dry ice bobbed up and down in the bottle. It looked a little like a small brown ocean with icebergs. The air in the bottle filled with white smoke, and some drifted lazily from the top.

Haley waited a couple of minutes before pouring a small amount into a cup. She did not want to accidentally get an ice burn, so she checked to make sure there were no pieces in the cup before lifting it to her lips. She swirled a small taste of soda around in her mouth and spat it in the sink. The root beer was still flat.

Now she was unsure about her idea. Why didn't it work? Had she been mistaken? A variety of thoughts bounced around inside her head.

Then it hit her. Of course, she thought, when soda is brand new, the bubbles are not visible until the cap is opened and the pressure inside the bottle is released. Haley had left the cap off during her experiment. She realized it was possible the open top let the carbon dioxide escape. Perhaps if she closed the cap and let the pressure build, the carbon dioxide would stay in the root beer. It might take time, but it should work.

Haley used the meat tenderizer to break more pieces from the dry ice and the paper funnel to get the ice into the bottle. She screwed the cap on tightly. With both hands she squeezed the bottle to see how much pressure there was initially. Her plan was to wait a few more minutes and squeeze it again to see if the pressure started to build.

While she waited, Haley carefully wrapped the remaining ice and placed it back under the fish in the cooler. She made sure all the utensils were put away and the counter clean. After a couple of minutes, she squeezed the bottle again. It did feel firmer to her. Her idea seemed to be working.

Haley decided it was better to let the bottle sit overnight before opening it again to see if the fizz was back in. She placed the bottle in the refrigerator on one of the metal racks toward the rear. As she closed the refrigerator door, she was feeling more optimistic her experiment would work.

That evening, the Bellamy family gathered around the dinner table together as they did every evening. The fish from the ice cooler were the main course. Mr. Bellamy cooked the entire dinner. His preparation of the fish took a long time. After filleting the fish, he rinsed and patted the fillets dry. The next step was to dip the fillets into flour, then egg, then bread crumbs before frying them briefly in a pan of butter and lemon. Haley had to admit the fish tasted wonderful and her father was an excellent fish chef. After dinner, J.R. and Mrs. Bellamy cleaned the counters while Haley cleared the table.

Twice during the evening, once just before dinner, and again just after, Haley checked on her experiment in the refrigerator. The bottle did seem quite a bit firmer, but she resisted the temptation to open it.

Haley checked it again one final time before it was time to go to bed. The bottle was definitely firmer. During her bedtime prayers, Haley added, "…and help my experiment to work. Amen." She adjusted the cross around her neck so it would be more comfortable during the night. Within minutes, she was fast asleep.

∾ CHAPTER 3 ∾

The Big Blast

KABOOM!

The explosion shook the house. Haley had been sleeping along the edge of her bed, and the sound of the explosion made her roll right off and hit the floor with a thump.

Einstein had been sleeping on the foot of her bed. He started barking wildly.

The sound of the explosion was quickly followed by the wailing of the house alarm and the sound of her mother screaming, "What was that!" She heard her father shouting, "J.R.! Haley! Everybody out!"

He burst into Haley's room, scooped her from the floor and swept her into his arms, before turning again and swiftly running down the hall and stairs. Einstein followed. From her vantage point in her father's arms, Haley could see J.R. just ahead with her mother.

The noise was terrific. The alarm continued to wail. Einstein barked. Mrs. Bellamy yelled at J.R. to stop pushing. J.R. was saying, "Stay calm. Stay calm," but did not seem to be acting calm. Mr. Bellamy was shouting, "Out, out! Go, go, go!"

Down the stairs, straight out the front door, and onto the front lawn they went. There they stopped and stood, shaking. Mr. Bellamy set Haley down on her feet. Mrs. Bellamy hugged Haley and J.R. Einstein went from person to person, almost as though he were checking to see if everyone was all right. Haley kneeled, and Einstein buried his head under her arm.

Less than a minute later, the clamor of sirens filled the night air. Einstein started barking again. A bright red fire truck with flashing red and blue lights pulled up and stopped. Two firefighters jumped out in full gear. One was lean and wiry. The other was slightly taller but beefy.

"Is anyone still inside the house?" the wiry firefighter asked.

Mr. Bellamy shook his head. "No. We're all out here and accounted for."

"Do you know what happened?"

Mr. Bellamy shook his head again, "There was this big explosion. The alarm went off. We didn't look to see what happened. We just got out of the house as quick as we could. Maybe a gas line ignited."

The tall beefy firefighter said, "If that was it, the house would be engulfed in flames. I don't see smoke escaping. We'll take a look inside."

With that, the two firefighters disappeared into the house. The Bellamys waited outside. They still shivered, but now more from the cold than the shock of the explosion. In less than five minutes, the firefighters came out from the house. Their oxygen masks dangled from the lanyards around their necks. The tall, beefy firefighter had a strange look on his face.

The wiry firefighter spoke first. "There was an explosion, just as you thought," he said. He continued, "The good news is the explosion was not a gas line or anything flammable."

"If it wasn't something flammable, then what was it?" J.R. asked.

The wiry firefighter hesitated. He opened his mouth to speak, but closed it again. His mouth puckered like a fish. Twice he tried to speak, but stopped

The tall firefighter spoke up. He still had the strange look on his face. "Well…uh…it seems your refrigerator was the cause of the explosion."

Mr. Bellamy, Mrs. Bellamy, and J.R. stared incredulously at him. They responded in chorus, "Our refrigerator?"

Now the reason for the firefighter's strange look became clear. He was trying very hard not to laugh. He forced himself to cough and tried to adopt a serious expression. "Actually," he said, "the refrigerator itself didn't explode. It was something inside the refrigerator that exploded."

"Inside?" they sang in unison.

A sinking feeling overcame Haley. She was still kneeling next to Einstein but happened to be slightly behind her father, out of view. She wished she could suddenly transform herself into a dog like Einstein.

Coughing again to stop from laughing, the tall firefighter said, "Yes —inside. We think we know which item in the refrigerator caused the explosion." He held up the remnants of a two-liter root beer plastic bottle.

"Can't say I've ever seen a root beer explosion like this before," he said. "It blew the door right off one of the hinges. The cap from the bottle shot right through the top of the refrigerator, and the bottom of the bottle drove a hole right through two metal racks. These plastic bottles are strong. My guess is that something created tremendous pressure inside the bottle, and when the plastic finally failed it acted just like an explosion. I just can't think of anything that could do that. Did somebody tamper with the bottle?"

Mr. Bellamy, Mrs. Bellamy, and J.R. remained frozen for several seconds. Then, almost as if on cue, they all turned and stared at Haley. The firefighters looked past where the Bellamys were standing to see who they were staring at.

The tall firefighter doubled over in laughter. "I knew it," he said glee-fully to his partner. He punched the wiry firefighter in the shoulder. "I told you I thought this was Haley Bellamy's house. I was right. Okay, now pay up!" He held out his hand.

The wiry firefighter dug deep inside his protective pants, pulled out a one dollar bill, and slapped it into the tall firefighter's hand. "Yeah, you were right."

"I was just trying to get the fizz back in the soda bottle," Haley said weakly.

Mr. Bellamy pressed his hand against his forehead and pushed back his hair. "What did you do?" he said, sounding exasperated.

Haley could feel her bottom lip starting to quiver. "I used some of the dry ice that was keeping the fish cold. I chipped off a bunch of small pieces and put them in the bottle to make it so it wouldn't be flat. I guess it worked, sort of."

The tall firefighter interrupted further questions. "Since it seems there isn't a fire and no one is hurt, we probably ought to get going."

The two firefighters gathered their equipment and headed for the truck. As they passed the Bellamy's, the tall one leaned over to Haley and whispered, "Sorry, Haley. Good luck."

After the firefighters left, the Bellamys and Einstein went back into the house. As they entered the kitchen, they could see the remains of the explosion. The door of the refrigerator hung oddly from one hinge. Food littered the floor. Red, yellow, and white splotches from broken cat-sup, mustard, and mayonnaise jars covered cabinet doors. Yogurt dripped from a twisted piece of shelving. Dishes were in splinters.

Haley felt a tear wet her cheek. "I'm sorry. I'm really sorry," was all she could think to say.

Mr. Bellamy leaned his head against the wall and closed his eyes. J.R. peered inside the broken door.

Mrs. Bellamy put her arm around Haley's shoulder. "Don't worry. The most important thing is that nobody was hurt. That by itself is a blessing," she said. "There's nothing more we can do this evening. Let's go to bed and we'll worry about this tomorrow."

Haley lay in her bed on her side, clutching her pillow to her chest. Einstein curled against her back and made soft dog snoring noises. The thought of the ruined refrigerator was firmly imprinted in Haley's mind. A tear formed and her eyes welled again.

She felt terrible. Despite her mother's earlier words, she was sure both her parents were furious. How could they not be? The refrigerator was ruined, the kitchen a mess. Fire trucks had come. It was going to be expensive to repair the damage.

A quiet knock at her door caught her attention. It was her mother. Mrs. Bellamy sat on the edge of Haley's bed and gently stroked her hair. Then Haley really began to cry.

"You're mad at me. So is Dad," she said between sobs.

Mrs. Bellamy looked directly at Haley. "No," she said, "I'm not angry. Your Dad is not angry either. We meant it when we said the most important thing was that you and J.R. were safe. We can replace a refrigerator. We can't replace you or J.R."

"I cause so much trouble," she sobbed. "Every time I try to fix something, it always goes wrong. I'm a lousy scientist. I should stop trying to be a scientist. You don't want me to be a scientist anyway."

Mrs. Bellamy hugged Haley tightly. "That's not true, honey," she soothed. "I admit that I don't know much about science or engineering, so I don't always understand what you're trying to do. But that doesn't

mean that you shouldn't pursue your interests."

Einstein stood and stretched. He yawned, circled three times, and lay down again.

Haley rubbed her face against her mother's shoulder. "I'm still a lousy scientist," she cried.

"You're a good scientist," Mrs. Bellamy responded. "True, things don't always work out like you want. But isn't that just part of science? Haven't you told me before, 'There's no such thing as a failed experiment, only a disproved hypothesis?' Besides, there's another reason you should continue your science efforts."

Haley sounded skeptical, "Why?"

Mrs. Bellamy gave a reassuring smile, "Because your love of science is a gift.[1] Everybody has different gifts. God gave you the gift of an inquiring and intelligent mind, and a wonderful love and understanding of science. It would be terrible if you didn't use the wonderful gifts you were given." She added, "Don't give up your gifts. Please think about it."

Mrs. Bellamy kissed Haley goodnight on the forehead and left. Haley snuggled closer to Einstein and thought about her mother's advice. Finally, just before she fell asleep, she nodded to herself. "I am a scientist," she thought.

1. Romans 12:6-8

❧ CHAPTER 4 ❧

The CATT Club

The next morning, Haley rode her bike to school. Now that the season had moved into fall, there were only a few weeks left that she could ride. Already, the mornings were cold enough that Haley's ears turned pink while riding. Soon, temperatures would drop further and snow on the ground would make it difficult and miserable to ride. But for now, the mornings were bearable and the afternoons were still warm and pleasant. She liked being able to zoom through fallen leaves, causing them to flutter and swirl in her wake.

Haley arrived at her school earlier than normal. The exploding refrigerator and fire trucks were bound to be news. Arriving earlier meant fewer people. With luck she might be able to avoid most kids and possibly sneak into the building unnoticed. Her plan was to go straight to her classroom and stay inside during the recess periods. She thought visiting the library or the computer lab were the best options.

She pulled up to the bike rack and swung off her bike while sliding her book bag from her shoulder to the ground. After squatting to lock her bike, she remained crouched for several moments and looked around.

Kinsley Bingham Elementary School was over 50 years old. In fact,

Haley's mother had attended the school as a girl. It was named after one of Michigan's most famous politicians, Kinsley Scott Bingham, who had served as a congressman, senator, and was a state governor in the 1850s.

The school looked its age. It was a low, one-story building built in the shape of a long H. The red brick exterior was weathered and worn. The windows that lined the building were old, thin, and un-insulated. In the winter, the heat was turned off during the weekends to save energy and not turned back on until just before Monday classes. Haley always shivered the first hour or so until the furnace warmed the rooms.

She scanned the area once more before rising to sneak inside. There were a few children on the play structure, taking the opportunity to play before class. A small group of boys were in the middle of the playground but were preoccupied with pushing and chasing each other. A brown-haired girl Haley did not know stood by herself at the far corner of the building. A teacher leaned against one wall near the main entrance drinking from a mug. There were few others. Haley decided to stay away from the girl and the teacher, and instead use a side entrance just around the corner closest to the bike rack.

Just before she stood, she heard the squeak of bicycle brakes behind her. It was Red.

Red jumped off her bike before it fully stopped. "Hi Haley," she said brightly. "Did the Cheese Puffs taste fishy?"

It was clear to Haley that Red did not know. "I guess you didn't hear," Haley said, ignoring the Cheese Puff question.

"Hear what?" Red asked looking puzzled. Red shifted her book bag. "Did the Cheese Puffs make you sick or something?"

"No, I didn't get sick," said Haley in a gloomy tone. "I wish it was that."

Red looked concerned. "Are you okay?" she asked. "You sound kinda

down. What's wrong?"

Haley glanced right and left. No one else was within hearing distance. She whispered, "I blew up the refrigerator."

Red's eyes widened. "Really?"

Haley nodded

Red adjusted her glasses. She lowered her voice, "You mean…little blow up, or big blow up?"

Haley pointed skyward with her thumb. She silently mouthed the word *big*.

"Cool!" Red said loudly.

The teacher leaning against the building looked in their direction. Haley grimaced.

Noticing Haley's face, Red said more quietly, "I mean, *cool*. How'd it happen?"

Haley told her.

As she listened carefully, the expression on Red's face went from excitement, to shock, to understanding. "Wow. That's amazing. You can't blame yourself. How could you know the dry ice would make the bottle of root beer explode? It was an accident. But, I can see why you don't want too many people to see you today," she said. "Don't worry, let's get inside. I'll help you find a good reason to stay inside during recess."

Haley and Red finished locking their bikes and moved to the corner of the building. Just before they reached it, three girls appeared from around the corner and blocked their path. It was the CATT Club!

The CATT Club took its name from the initials of the last names of the girls in the club. There were Cynthia Clarke, Andrea (pronounced with a long emphasis on the *An* so it sounded like *Aaannndrea*) Alger, Victoria Tachikawa, and Julie Tanner. All the members of the CATT Club were one year older than Haley and Red and in the fifth grade.

Julie Tanner had moved away at the beginning of the school year, but the CATT Club had kept the club name with two *T*'s anyway. The CATT Club mostly worked hard at being bossy, pushy, and mean, as well as generally excluding other kids from any CATT Club activities.

The leader of the CATT Club was Cynthia. She spoke first. "Well," she sneered loudly, "if it isn't the brainy scientist and her freckled companion." Cynthia always spoke loudly. She crossed her arms.

Following Cynthia's lead, Victoria and Andrea crossed their arms. Victoria piped up. "Don't you mean her flaming companion? Hair like that could start a fire without matches."

Red inhaled deeply. Her mouth started working as though words were being formed and would burst forth any second.

Haley put her hand on Red's elbow to caution her. Responding to the CATT Club with anger never worked anyway, it would just make the situation worse. It was better to ignore their comments and get away as soon as possible. Besides, Haley knew she and Red were viewed as neutral for the most part. Better to stay that way than invite the wrath of the CATT Club.

"What do you want, Cynthia?" sighed Haley.

Andrea spoke instead. "We heard there were fire trucks at your house last night. What happened?" she asked sarcastically.

How did they know about that? Haley wondered if they knew more. She guessed they did not, but that they saw an opportunity to torment somebody. Haley shrugged her shoulders. "Oh…the house alarm went off. The firefighters came to check it out. That's all."

A choked laugh emitted from the CATT Club girls. Victoria shook her black hair. Her narrow eyes peered at Haley and Red from behind her black-rimmed glasses. "Are you sure that's what it was?" she mocked. "Or did Meredith's hair set your house on fire? Maybe we should call *her*

Torch."

Haley knew Red did not like being called by her formal name. She tightened her grip on Red's elbow.

Red was mad. "My name is Red," she said. "What do you really want anyway? It was just like Haley said. The alarm went off and the fire trucks came to check it out. That's it."

Cynthia's dark eyes flashed at Red, then glanced past the girls. Out of the corner of her eye, Haley could see what she was looking at. The teacher who had been leaning against the building near the entrance was now walking in their direction.

The CATT Club shifted past Haley and Red before the teacher reached them. As they moved off, Cynthia glanced over her shoulder. Her eyes darkened further. "You should be more careful around the house, Haley. You never know when something's going to *blow up*," she said.

Haley and Red hurried in the other direction before the teacher could reach them, and slipped inside the building.

"How'd she know already?" asked Haley breathlessly.

Red adjusted her glasses. "Who knows," she said. "But you can bet the entire school will hear about it before the first recess. Try not to worry about it."

"Yeah. Sure," agreed Haley. But she knew she was going to worry about it anyway.

Word of the exploding refrigerator spread like wildfire. As the story was told from person to person, it gradually changed and became more fantastic. Already, a story was going around that Haley had made a bomb that went off in the middle of the night and destroyed an entire city block with extensive casualties.

At the first recess, Haley was successful in her effort to stay inside.

With Red's help, she convinced her teacher, Mrs. Vasey, that she needed to spend the recess in the library to work on her country geography project. Red stayed with Haley in the library and tried to help her figure out a way to avoid the second recess.

Unfortunately, they were not successful and found themselves standing next to the school building at the edge of the playground. A crowd of children clustered around Haley and Red, wanting to hear more. The girls spent most of their time refuting the false stories. After a while, the crowd slowly melted away as the initial excitement waned. Finally, Haley and Red were left alone.

"You're very popular today," Red observed.

Haley frowned at Red. "Not popular in a good way. More like popular in the same way the polar bear is popular at the zoo. I feel like I'm on display for people to look at and gawk," she responded.

Red nodded her head in agreement and shrugged.

The girls stood in silence for a while and watched several younger children on the slide of the play set. Although the slide was fairly tall and steep, Haley noticed that the kids sliding down it were not sliding much at all. In fact, it seemed as though they were forced to push themselves down it. Without thinking, Haley started to rub her chin. She stared hard at the slide. Why were the children having so much trouble, she wondered.

Red was talking to her, but she did not notice. Haley started across the playground to the slide. Red was accustomed to this behavior. She stopped talking and followed Haley.

At the edge of the slide, Haley watched a first-grade boy try to go down it. He did not go down smoothly. He was forced to push himself to the bottom. It was almost as though his pants were sticking to the slide.

After he passed, Haley whipped out her magnifying glass and studied the surface of the slide. It was metal. The sides were slightly corroded and dull, but the middle part of the slide was shiny. She put her face close to the surface and peered through her magnifying glass. She expected to see a rough surface, but it was very smooth.

Her mind started to work furiously. She knew rough surfaces could cause more friction, so objects like the garbage can on the rough driveway would not slide easily. However, in this case the surface was smooth and she doubted the boy's pants would be the sole cause. She furrowed her eyebrows and thought hard. She wondered if there might be a way to make the slide work better.

"Maybe Aunt Gabby knows something about friction," she mumbled to herself.

"What about your aunt and friction?" Red asked.

Haley did not answer. She rubbed her chin harder and thought more.

Her thoughts were interrupted by a nudge from Red. Haley looked up. Red motioned with her head toward a girl standing near the playground fence on the other side of the slide. Haley did not know her, but recognized her. It was the same girl she had seen standing by herself when Haley arrived at school early in the morning.

The girl had dark hair pulled back into a single ponytail. Her brown eyes complemented a fine face with soft features. Her hands were clasped behind her back. She was standing by herself and seemed to be observing the activities on the playground.

Haley was curious. "I saw her this morning, but I don't think I have seen her at school before," she said. "Do you know her name? She must be new."

Red shook her head. "I've seen her a couple of times over the past week. I think she is new, but I don't know her name."

The girl noticed Haley and Red watching her and then looked off to her right. Haley and Red followed her gaze. Red said, "Uh-oh. Big trouble."

The CATT Club trio approached the new girl and stopped in front of her. The girls surrounded her. The new girl looked like she was trying to move away from the CATT Club, but each time she shifted, either Andrea or Victoria would shift with her to keep her boxed in. Haley strained to hear the conversation, but she could only hear when Cynthia spoke.

Haley heard bits and pieces like, "New girl…clod…orphan…clod… keep your place."

Finally, the CATT Club moved away. The new girl stood alone again. She looked shaken. Haley saw her steal a glance at them. Then she put her head down and walked swiftly toward the red brick school building.

After watching the entire episode, a feeling rose inside Haley. It was not a good feeling. "I wonder if I should have done something to help," she mumbled, mostly to herself.

Red adjusted her glasses. "Yeah. Maybe. But remember we don't know who she is or anything. Besides, you've already had a run-in with the CATT Club this morning. You said yourself, it's better to let it pass. Remember? As long as the new girl doesn't bother any of the CATT Club girls, she'll be okay."

"You might be right," Haley said. "But I still don't feel good."

The bell rang announcing the end of recess, and the girls headed to their classroom. Haley sighed and put her magnifying glass in her dress pocket. She still felt like she should have tried to help. She also was thinking about whether she could devise a way for the slide to work better. As she walked, she absentmindedly rubbed her chin.

∾ CHAPTER 5 ∾

A Samaritan Story

The first thing Haley noticed after she arrived home was the kitchen looked as though nothing had happened the evening before, except there was a suspiciously new-looking refrigerator in place of the old one. Her mother and J.R. were in the kitchen. Mrs. Bellamy was drying her hands on a towel. J.R. stood leaning against the kitchen counter, his nose buried in a skateboard magazine.

"Wow!" Haley exclaimed. "The kitchen doesn't look much different, except the refrigerator. Didn't the explosion damage anything?"

Mrs. Bellamy replied, "I was surprised too, but no. Of course, the explosion ruined the refrigerator, but the door didn't hit the cabinets when it blew off." She finished drying her hands and hung the towel over the handle of the oven door. She continued, "Your dad and I took the day off to work on the kitchen. I went shopping for a new refrigerator while your dad scrubbed the floor and cabinets. We were lucky the store was able to deliver it right away. Other than the refrigerator, it seems the only damage was a few new scuff marks on the floor."

"Wow, I'm glad nothing was broken," Haley said with relief.

Mrs. Bellamy excused herself for a minute, leaving Haley alone with

J.R. He was still leaning against the counter with his nose in the skateboard magazine. Haley looked around the kitchen. Her stomach grumbled. She noticed dinner had not been started. Since her mother worked part-time and her father finished his shift at the automotive plant by middle afternoon, the Bellamys usually had dinner on the table around 5:00 p.m.

Dinner duty rotated among the Bellamys. Today was Tuesday, so cooking dinner was J.R.'s responsibility.

Haley asked, "J.R., aren't you going to cook dinner?"

Without looking up from his magazine, he used a monotone voice to answer. "Already done. It's in the new refrigerator if you want to see it."

Haley tugged at the refrigerator door. This one took more effort to open than the old one. She tugged harder and finally the door swung open. She looked inside. The refrigerator was completely empty except for one thing. There was a single two-liter bottle of root beer standing by itself.

Behind Haley, the sound of laughter erupted. She turned. J.R.'s face was contorted with glee. Both the magazine in his hands and his shaggy brown hair shook from the force of his laughter.

"That's not funny. Stop laughing!" Haley demanded.

"It *is* funny," was his retort. "Exploding root beer, I love it! When I told my friends today, they didn't believe me at first. But I showed my buddy, Kenny, the old refrigerator when they were taking it away, then —"

A voice from the hallway interrupted him. It was Mrs. Bellamy returning. "J.R.!" she warned. Her tone left no room for interpretation. "That's enough! It's not funny! Someone could have easily been killed. Take that bottle out of there! That's cruel and uncalled for. Haley feels bad enough. Just drop it."

J.R. looked taken aback at his mother's strong rebuff. "Ah, c'mon Mom, it was just a joke. I was trying to be humorous."

"Well, it wasn't funny, J.R. Besides, we're supposed to leave it empty and closed for 24 hours before we put any food in it," Mrs. Bellamy said.

"Take the bottle out," she repeated, "and go upstairs and clean your room. Aunt Gabby is coming over tonight and I want the house reasonably clean."

J.R. did not say anything more. He exhaled deeply, slumped his shoulders, and bobbed his head as he started from the kitchen. As he passed Haley, he turned his face to her and bared his teeth in a grimace.

Haley frowned back.

"Mom," Haley said, "if we can't put food in there for another day, what're we going to do for dinner tonight?"

"Your dad is running a couple of errands right now. He's going to pick up some pizza on his way back," Mrs. Bellamy explained.

That was good news. Pizza was one of Haley's favorite foods, but was a rare treat. Mrs. Bellamy often noted it was more expensive to eat out than to cook.

A thought pushed into Haley's mind. It was something that had been bothering her most of the day. She was still thinking about the new girl at school and the CATT Club. Now that Haley was alone with her mother, she could ask her opinion. "Mom, can I ask you about something?"

Mrs. Bellamy stared at her. Haley knew her mother was mildly surprised at her request. After all, it was fairly unusual for Haley to voluntarily ask her mother's opinion. She did so only when something was really bothering her.

"Sure. Why don't we sit down at the table," Mrs. Bellamy suggested.

After they were settled, Mrs. Bellamy said, "I hope you're not worrying

anymore about the refrigerator."

Haley shook her head. "I'm still a little worried about that, but this is different. I saw something happen at school today, but didn't do anything. Now I'm wondering if I should have."

"Can you tell me what happened?" Mrs. Bellamy asked.

Each end of the family table was hinged so the ends could be left up if they had guests, or folded under if it were only the four Bellamys. The ends were in the up position because Aunt Gabby was expected later. Haley hesitated for a few seconds, running her finger along the table seam.

Finally, she started to tell about seeing the new girl at school and how the CATT Club had surrounded the girl. She also told what she had been able to overhear. "She must feel terrible, especially if she's an orphan or something," Haley said. "It's gotta be bad enough being new. She probably feels even worse after being pushed around by the CATT Club."

A few moments of silence ensued. Haley could tell her mother was thinking and tried to read the expression on her face.

"I'm glad you were thinking about it," said Mrs. Bellamy. "You've heard the expression *Love your neighbor as yourself*?"[2]

Haley nodded.

Mrs. Bellamy went further. "Do you remember what that is supposed to mean?"

Haley had not thought much about it before. She tried to imagine what her mother meant. Haley was certain she was nice to her friends, like Red. There were also neighbors on both sides of the Bellamys. On one side were the Steinmetzes. They had two small babies. On the other side were the Jamals. Their children were already grown. The Bellamys were friendly with both neighbors. In fact, Mrs. Steinmetz said Haley

2. Luke 10:27

could babysit for them when she was a little older. "I guess it means that we should be nice to our friends and the people who live near us?" she suggested.

"It does mean that," agreed Mrs. Bellamy, "but it goes further. It's intended to mean that everyone around us is our neighbor, even strangers, and we should help them when we can."

The clicking of nails on the hard floor distracted Haley briefly. It was Einstein. Apparently, he had finally moved from his sleeping spot on the living room sofa. When he was younger, he would race to the front door to greet Haley when she returned home from school. These days, he only moved quickly if food was involved. He wagged his tail as Haley bent over to scratch behind his ears.

"Haley, let me tell you a story," Mrs. Bellamy said. Haley turned her attention back to her mother. "Once there was a man traveling between two towns. Along the way, some robbers found him. They took his money and beat him. He was so badly injured that he couldn't move. He just lay there by the side of the road." [3]

Haley's eyes widened. "What happened to him?"

"Good question," Mrs. Bellamy said. "Several people saw the injured man. One was a priest. When he saw the man, he actually went across the street to avoid him. Another man saw him, but didn't want to get involved. So he also crossed the street and stayed away. Finally, a stranger approached. He saw the man was injured and tried to help him. The stranger gave the injured man first aid, took him to the hospital, and even paid the medical bills."

Haley was impressed. "Is that a true story?" she wondered out loud.

Einstein jumped up onto Mrs. Bellamy's lap and licked her chin. It was the most energy he had expended the entire day. Mrs. Bellamy held

3. Luke 10:30-37

Einstein's head away from her face.

"Haley," said Mrs. Bellamy, sounding exasperated. "It's a well-known story from the Bible. There are also stories like this in the newspaper every day." She squinted. "Didn't you learn about this story in Sunday school? The Good Samaritan story—remember?"

Haley thought hard. She could easily rattle off the first twenty five elements from the periodic table, but had a more difficult time remembering what she learned in Sunday school. "Uh—no," she said.

A baffled looked crossed Mrs. Bellamy's face briefly, followed by a single nod and a small laugh. She pushed Einstein off her lap. "I can see we're going to need to put more focus on that. In any case, the point is that everyone is our neighbor, even strangers."

"I see your point, Mom," Haley agreed. "But what do you think I should do?"

Rising from her chair, Mrs. Bellamy said, "That will depend on the situation. You need to look out for your friends, but we also need to help strangers. It makes us better people. You could intervene. You could get help from a teacher. You could do something else. You'll need to evaluate and make your own decision for what makes the most sense. The main thing to remember is that you shouldn't ignore a problem just because it's happening to a stranger."

Haley remained at the table after her mother left. She thought about her mother's advice. Einstein put his paws on Haley's leg. She reached down and struggled to pull him onto her lap. He was heavy. She absentmindedly let Einstein lick her hand while she thought more about the conversation with her mother. Although she did not know exactly what she would do the next time the CATT Club bothered the new girl, she knew she would not idly stand by.

✑ CHAPTER 6 ✑

Friction

A low rumbling sound, similar to thunder from an approaching storm, interrupted Haley's thoughts. Haley could hear it coming from outside the front of the house. The rumble grew louder before steadying for a few seconds, then roared once before falling silent. The noise could mean only one thing: Aunt Gabby had arrived! Haley ran to the front door.

Before she could reach it, the door flew open and in strode her aunt. Aunt Gabby stopped when she saw Haley. "Hey girl!" she exclaimed.

Without another word, Haley and Aunt Gabby faced each other. They squared themselves and set their hands on their hips. Then they gave each other a high-fives with their right hands and high-fives with their left hands. Then they gave each other side-fives and low-fives. A loud crack was heard each time their palms smacked together. At the end, Haley squealed, "Aunt Gabby!" and gave her a fierce hug. Haley and her aunt greeted each other this way every time they met.

Haley's Aunt Gabby may have been a scientist, but she did not look like the typical scientist. Some people may have expected to see a dour-looking woman with glasses, hair wound into a neat bun, and wearing a boring suit. Aunt Gabby was just the opposite. She wore her hair spiky so it shot off into different directions. The other interesting thing about her hair was the color, or rather, the multiple colors. Aunt Gabby changed her hair color as often as some people changed clothes. It could be brown, blond, orange, purple, green, pink, or something else. Today it was blue. Like many scientists, she needed to wear glasses. Although she wore contact lenses most of the time, varying the color depending on her hair color. Today, she wore green cat-eyed lenses to complement her blue hair. She had on worn blue jeans, tennis shoes, and a leather bomber jacket over a white tank top. The rumbling Haley had heard was her aunt's convertible sports car with a powerful engine.

Aunt Gabby followed as Haley led the way to the kitchen. On the way, Aunt Gabby whispered, "I heard you had a little experiment go south."

Haley looked back at Aunt Gabby and grimaced. "More than south I think. It was not good. Definitely bad."

"They still mad?" Aunt Gabby asked, referring to Haley's parents.

"No," Haley replied. "That's the weird thing. They get upset if I spill juice or something, so I was scared they'd be really, really angry. But, they didn't get that mad about this. They just seemed to be glad no one got hurt." Haley shrugged her shoulders. "Maybe they're saving up their frustration and they will get mad sometime later. You know, I've heard about delayed reactions."

Aunt Gabby grinned. "I don't think you need to be concerned about that. If they aren't mad now, they won't be later," she said. She winked and continued. "Nope. I think your folks just showed they have their priorities right."

As they entered the kitchen, Einstein greeted Aunt Gabby with whines and tail wags. He flopped down and rolled onto his back. Aunt Gabby rubbed his belly and scratched under his chin. "Einstein, you're looking a bit grayer around the muzzle every time I see you."

Aunt Gabby stood and surveyed the room. "Other than the new refrigerator, no obvious damage," she said. "I would've loved to have seen the bottle and refrigerator after the explosion. I should set up an experiment at the office to measure the explosive force and direction—" She was interrupted before she could finish.

"Gabby!" It was Mrs. Bellamy.

"Hi Liz," said Aunt Gabby. Her green cat eyes had an amused look. "Haley and I were just talking about your refrigerator and how lucky you were to have a reason to get a new one. I bet this one is even more energy efficient than the last one. You'll probably save money on your electric bill."

Mrs. Bellamy looked sharply at Haley.

Haley's face looked panicked. She shook her head and waved her hands in front of her trying to signal she did not think it lucky at all.

"I'm just kidding of course. By the way, where's my little brother?" Aunt Gabby asked. Haley's father was two years younger than Aunt Gabby, who often reminded him of that fact.

The strained look left Mrs. Bellamy's face once she realized it was a joke. However, it was clear she did not think the joke was funny. Her reply sounded defensive. "I knew you were just trying to be funny. Ha. Ha. Of course, it's funny now, but the big *boom* and fire trucks weren't funny at the time. Anyway, John is still out. He's running some errands, but is planning to bring back pizza."

Mrs. Bellamy raised one eyebrow as though a thought had entered her head. "I've got an idea. Why don't you take Haley and get the pizza. I'll call John on his cell phone and let him know. I think he's running behind anyway, so it'll be one less errand for him. We'll also get dinner done earlier that way. Let me give you some money for the pizza."

Haley hoped her aunt would agree. It would give her a chance to talk with Aunt Gabby about friction.

A mischievous gleam shone from Aunt Gabby's eyes as she squinted at Mrs. Bellamy. "Tell you what," she said. "I'll buy the pizza, but I get to choose the kind."

Haley looked back and forth at her mother and Aunt Gabby. Their exchange was almost like a ping-pong ball being batted back and forth over a net. How would it end?

"No fishies and no onions, otherwise anything you want," Mrs. Bellamy countered.

"Deal," Aunt Gabby said. "We're outa here and back in a flash." She winked at Haley. "Let's roll, girl."

The top was already down on Aunt Gabby's sports car. Haley settled herself into the passenger seat. She loved to ride in her aunt's car. It was low, sleek, and red with only two doors and two seats. The seats were firm but comfortable. The sides of the seat curled around Haley's shoulders, hips, and legs giving her a secure cocoon feeling.

Aunt Gabby slipped into the driver's seat and donned a pair of thin leather driving gloves that had been lying on the center console.

"Remember your seat belt," Aunt Gabby said. "Better to stay with the car than fly out of it, I always say."

Haley reached over her shoulder for her seat belt and grasped at air momentarily before she remembered this car had very different seat belts. Instead, Haley used both hands, reached directly behind her neck, and pulled two thick straps down either side of her shoulders. She snapped each strap into a center piece that came up from the middle of the seat between her legs. She then pulled two lap belts across her waist and snapped them into the center piece also. Haley remembered her aunt called the seat belt a five-point harness.

Aunt Gabby nodded and said, "Yep, I do that too after I've been driving somebody else's car." She leaned over and checked that Haley's seat belt was snug. Then she reached across Haley, opened the glove compartment, and pulled out two baseball caps. She jammed one on Haley's head and put the other on her own head. "Keeps the hair out of our eyes," she noted.

The engine started to life with a low throaty rumble. Haley could feel the vibration as the engine murmured. They pulled away from the curb swiftly. The temperature had already begun to drop. Haley could feel the cold on her ears. She was glad she had grabbed her mother's heavy sweater before leaving the house.

"Aunt Gabby, do you know much about friction?" Haley asked in a voice loud enough to be heard over the noise of the wind and the car's engine.

Aunt Gabby leaned in Haley's direction. "I specialize in lasers and optics, but I know a fair amount about friction. What'd you want to know?"

"Well, I know the word *friction* and that it basically means when two things rub against each other," Haley replied.

A traffic light ahead turned red. Aunt Gabby slowed the car to a stop. "That's more or less right. Friction is really the force, the amount of effort, needed to move one thing when it is in contact with another. For example, if I have a brick lying on the ground, there is friction where the brick contacts the ground. Friction is the amount of force needed to get the brick to move and keep it moving."

"Do rough surfaces create more friction?" Haley asked.

"Not necessarily," Aunt Gabby explained. "Even a really smooth surface can create a lot of friction. Race car tires have smooth surfaces, but have a really strong grip on the road. Here, let me show you."

The light turned green. Aunt Gabby revved the engine to a thunderous roar before she suddenly released the brake. The convertible shot forward. Haley felt herself pushed back deep against the seat. Her vision blurred briefly.

"See, the tires didn't squeal or even chirp." Aunt Gabby shouted over the roar. She eased off the gas. The car slowed somewhat.

Haley gasped. "Wow!"

Aunt Gabby pointed. The pizza place was just ahead. She said, "Let's see if we can break loose these tires by braking. Hang on!" She stomped on the brakes.

Haley slammed against the seat belt straps as the car stopped even faster than it accelerated. She was glad she was wearing the five-point seat belt instead of a regular shoulder harness. The car ride was getting a bit too exciting, even for Haley.

Aunt Gabby slapped her hand against the steering wheel, "Rats! I forgot. This thing's got anti-lock brakes. Sorry Haley, no tire squeaks today."

"That's okay," Haley mumbled. She felt a little dizzy.

The car turned into the parking lot. Aunt Gabby guided the car into a parking spot right in front of the sign that read *Mercury Pizza*. Underneath in smaller words it said *Pizza so good it's out of this world*. She let the car idle a while longer.

Haley had another question. "How do you know how much force is needed?"

Taking off her leather driving gloves, Aunt Gabby said, "Good question. Every object is different. It's actually pretty complex. It depends on several factors: the weight of the object, the material it's made from, how much of the surface is in contact, and so forth. There is something called the coefficient of friction, which is a number that tells you how

much force is needed. The amount of force is also different depending on whether the object is already moving or not. In fact, it takes more effort to start something moving and less effort once it is already moving. Each is called by a different name. Static friction is the force needed to get something moving. Kinetic friction is the force needed to keep something moving once it has started. You can actually try it. Take something somewhat heavy and push against it. You'll see that you don't have to push as hard once it's moving."

Haley remembered her struggle with the garbage can. Aunt Gabby was right. It took less effort to keep the garbage can moving once it started. "Is there any way to make the friction less?" Haley asked.

"Sure. A good example is the oil used in car engines. Oil helps reduce friction. It also helps keep the engine cooler. If an engine ran out of oil, more friction and heat would be created until the engine finally stopped," said Aunt Gabby. She grasped the key and turned. The engine fell silent.

Haley frowned. Maybe engine oil could be the answer for the slide at school, she thought. However, she knew there was no way she was going to get her hands on some.

She rubbed her chin and thought furiously. An idea was beginning to form. Then a light went on in Haley's mind. "Would something like vegetable oil also reduce friction?" she asked.

Aunt Gabby reached over and released Haley's seat belt. "Probably not in a car engine, but vegetable oil would generally work if you didn't have to worry about heat. The main idea is to create a thin layer of something slippery between the two objects to reduce the friction."

Haley nodded. She thought vegetable oil just might work. It certainly should help reduce the friction on the slide. But how could she get it to school? It would not make sense to haul an entire bottle on her bicycle.

Perhaps a small plastic squeeze bottle would work better. She remembered seeing some small bottles in the camping box in the garage. She would need to check after they returned home. Haley felt really good— her problem was solved!

They got out of the car and entered the pizza store. Behind the counter stood a college-aged girl. "Can I help you?" she said.

Aunt Gabby turned to Haley and asked, "Which toppings am I not allowed to order?"

"Anchovies and onions is what Mom said."

"That's what I thought," observed Aunt Gabby. She turned back to the girl and smiled. "We would like to order two large pepperoni, pickle, and raisin pizzas," she said.

Haley's eyes widened. *Oh no,* she thought.

CHAPTER 7

An Enemy of the CATT Club

Haley woke up to the sound of her alarm clock. It was Wednesday morning. She had set her alarm early so she could get the vegetable oil without scrutiny by her mother or J.R. She was not worried about her father. Even at that early hour, she knew he had left long before because his shift at the automotive plant started at 6:00 a.m.

When her mother came downstairs, she appeared mildly surprised to see Haley already dressed, sitting at the table eating breakfast, with her book bag ready and waiting by the door. But she did not question it. Haley made it out the door with the small plastic squeeze bottle of vegetable oil safety tucked in the side pocket of her book bag. Her plan was to swing by Red's house so they could ride to school together.

As Haley rode her bicycle, she noticed the weather was definitely colder than earlier in the week. Granted most of the leaves had already fallen off the trees and were still on the ground, but it seemed as though winter was coming faster than normal. She could feel the cold bite her ears.

Red's house was about four blocks from Haley's, but not directly on the way to school. When Haley pulled up, Red was already waiting on the sidewalk in front of her house. Haley could see Red was wearing muffs over her ears and wished she had some.

They rode on the sidewalk toward the school. "Did ya talk with your Aunt Gabby last night about friction?" Red asked.

Even while riding, Haley could see the frost from her breath before it whipped away. "Yep. I've got a little bottle of vegetable oil with me," she said.

They stopped at the corner and dismounted before walking their bicycles across the intersection. Red adjusted her glasses with one hand. "Vegetable oil?" she asked. "She said to use vegetable oil on the slide?"

"Not exactly," Haley said. "We didn't talk specifically about the slide, but more about friction in general. She said vegetable oil would help reduce it."

"Vegetable oil?" Red repeated. "Do you think it's a good idea to use that at school?"

They got on their bicycles and started to ride again. "Sure," Haley said firmly. "I'll only use a little and besides, a slide that doesn't slide isn't any fun for anybody."

A skeptical look crossed Red's face, but she said, "Okay. You're the scientist."

Even with the cold, kids were milling around the school building and on the playground when Haley and Red stopped next to the bike rack. They hopped off their bikes and pushed them into adjacent racks. Before they had a chance to lock their bikes, Red nudged Haley. "Hey, look," she said.

Immediately Haley could see what Red meant. The new brown-haired girl was standing at the same far corner of the school building where she had been the morning before. Only this time, she was surrounded by the CATT Club.

The CATT Club had closed in around her like they had the day before, with Cynthia in front and Andrea and Victoria blocking the brown-haired girl's attempts to get away. Haley could see they crowded her even more this time. The girl held her hands in front of her, but Cynthia bumped her shoulder against the girl anyway.

A panicked feeling rose in Haley. She quickly looked around her. No teachers were visible. Usually there was a parent volunteer or two near the school entrance, but not this time. She thought about the crossing guard in front of the school, but she was too far away to see what was happening. No one else seemed to notice or care about the girl's predicament.

What should she do? Like an echo, her conversation with her mother sounded through her mind. "You shouldn't ignore a problem just because it's happening to a stranger," she remembered her mother saying. She recalled her own promise to herself that she would not idly stand by. Of course, it felt far easier to make that promise when she had been sitting safely at the kitchen table.

Haley tried to think. It would take time to find a teacher in the building and get the teacher outside. Perhaps the crossing guard was an option? Then she realized the crossing guard could not leave the busy street for safety reasons. The only thing Haley could figure out was to intervene herself.

The idea frightened her. Cynthia, Andrea, and Victoria were bigger and older. Haley had never heard of the CATT Club actually punching someone, but she imagined they might if sufficiently provoked. The thought of being punched frightened her even more.

She closed her eyes and prayed silently, "God, I know I need to help the girl, but I'm really scared. Give me the courage to be brave enough to help her...please...Amen."

Her eyes blinked open. She still felt very scared, but her mind was focused.

"Let's go," she said. Her tone was serious. She started walking toward the girl and the CATT Club.

Red looked at Haley in surprise. "Let's go where?" she asked, but followed anyway.

"This way," Haley ordered.

They were heading directly toward the CATT Club. Red looked confused and squinted at Haley. "Yesterday you said to let it pass."

Haley shook her head. "I was wrong. I'm not crossing the street to the other side again," she said.

Red looked even more confused, but then a new fire burned in her eyes. She pushed her gold-rimmed glasses firmly on her nose. "I have no idea what you just said, but I know what you want to do. I'm with you all the way."

As they approached, they could see the new girl had started to cry. The CATT Club's backs were to them. Haley heard Victoria saying, "You crying because you're an orphan or because you're a clod?" Victoria reached out and knocked a book out of the girl's hand.

Haley's heart thumped wildly. She could feel it pounding in her chest. She was still scared, but also a little mad. Haley and Red stopped a few feet behind the CATT Club. Haley did not want her voice to waver or crack, so she took a deep breath before she spoke.

"That's enough. Leave her alone." Her voice was stronger than she expected.

Cynthia wheeled about. She scowled when she saw Haley and Red. Victoria and Andrea also looked in their direction. "What did you say?" Cynthia asked menacingly.

Haley swallowed hard. "I said that's enough. She's not done anything to you. Leave her alone."

A look came over Victoria's face. "Why do you care? You don't know her. She's an orphan and a nobody," she sneered.

Andrea chimed in, "Yeah. Just walk away. No harm, no foul if you go away now."

The fire was still in Red's eyes. She had been waiting her turn. "No harm, no foul," she repeated sarcastically. "What does *that* mean? Look. We're here. We're not leaving. Leave her alone."

"You may be here," growled Cynthia, "but what're you going to do?"

Without another word, Haley squeezed between Cynthia and Victoria and stood next to the new girl. She brushed against Cynthia hard enough to make her take a step to the side. Red followed her lead and squeezed through the other side, between Cynthia and Andrea, and stood on the other side of the new girl.

Haley crossed her arms in defiance. "I don't know what we're going to do, but we're not leaving," she said.

Andrea and Victoria stared at Haley and Red with uncertainty. No one had ever stood up to the CATT Club before. No one. They both looked at Cynthia.

A hurt and surprised look flashed across Cynthia's face. She took another step backward. Her face was contorted and red. She breathed in sharply, twice, before she spoke. "You've made an enemy of the CATT Club. Both of you! Now's not the time, but you, Boom Boom Root Beer," she said, pointing at Haley, "and you, Torch," pointing at Red, "had better watch it. This is going to cost you plenty." With that, Cynthia wheeled about and stormed off with Andrea and Victoria in her wake.

Haley could not believe it. It had worked! The CATT Club was gone, at least for now. Her pounding heart began to slow its wild thumping. Her arms felt shaky. She leaned her head back, breathed deeply, and closed her eyes just briefly enough to whisper a silent prayer. "Thank

you, Lord, that I didn't get beat up."

"Yay, Haley!" exclaimed Red. She bounced in front of Haley and the new girl, pumped her fist, and said, "Yesss!"

The new girl had stopped crying but was still sniffing. Haley turned to her and asked, "Are you okay?"

"I think so. I still feel a little scared. Thanks for your help," she said. Her voice trembled. She also had a slight accent, but Haley could not place it.

Red replied, "Don't mention it. Why have they been bugging you? Did you do anything to them?"

"I didn't do anything. Maybe it's `cause I'm new. Since I got here three weeks ago, they've bothered me a couple of other times. I told my teacher the first time, but it got a lot worse right away after that."

Red nodded. "That explains it. I bet your teacher talked with them the first time and now they're mad at you for getting them in trouble."

Haley reached down, picked up the book from the ground, and handed it to the girl. "My name's Haley," she said. "And this," she motioned, "is Red."

The new girl's voice began to sound stronger. "I'm Claudia Valencia."

A look of comprehension crossed Red's face. "Claudia? Ah…that explains why they kept calling you *Clod*. The CATT Club can take anyone's name and twist it. They're not nice girls. That's especially mean that they made fun of you, being an orphan and all."

Claudia's soft features hardened a bit. "I'm not an orphan," she declared solidly.

"Sorry." Red was taken aback. "I didn't mean anything by it. Why do you think they keep calling you an orphan if you're not one?"

Claudia sighed. "It's probably because I'm staying with my grandmother for now. My parents are living overseas for a while."

"Why are they doing that?" Haley asked.

The bell rang. The girls headed for the school entrance. Claudia answered as they walked. "My parents are diplomats for Mexico. We used to live in San Francisco, but we moved back to Mexico City a year ago. Last month, my parents were posted to Chad in Africa. My dad is an ambassador now and my mom is the cultural attaché. They said Chad was too dangerous for kids. My grandmother moved here about three years ago. So I have to stay here with her. They'll be there for two years."

"Your parents are diplomats!" said Red. "That's cool."

Claudia frowned slightly. "I suppose. I've never really thought about it. The bad part is I won't be able to see them for two years."

Nodding, Red agreed, "I guess it's not as great when you put it that way."

Haley tried to imagine if her own parents went away for two years. What would that be like? She was sure it would be difficult. She felt even better for helping Claudia get away from the CATT Club. It must've been hard enough being new to a school and knowing your parents would be gone for two years, let alone having the CATT Club single you out. Haley decided to cheer Claudia up. "Don't worry," she said. "The two years will go fast with friends like us! We'll walk with you to your class. We can meet again at recess. I've got an experiment I need to try."

Claudia's face brightened. "That'd be great," she said, "but I don't get the part about the experiment."

Red patted her on the back and grinned broadly. "Not to worry," she assured her. "Welcome to the world of Haley. It's full of surprises and always exciting!"

∾ CHAPTER 8 ∾

The Oil Solution

Before the first recess, Haley had switched the squeeze bottle from her book bag to the pocket of her jeans. She also grabbed a couple of paper towels from the classroom sink and jammed those into a back pocket.

At recess, the girls met in the hallway and went outside to the playground. It was still cool, but bright sun made the air feel warmer. Haley headed straight for the slide. Red and Claudia trailed behind. Claudia asked, "Where're we going?"

Haley did not answer. She was so absorbed in her thoughts about the slide that she barely heard Claudia's question. Although she knew she was going to try to see if the vegetable oil would reduce the friction of the slide, she had not fully worked out what she was going to do. Should she simply put the oil on, or should she see if the friction problem was different from the day before? If it was still a problem, should she put on a lot of oil, or just a small amount? Haley rubbed her chin furiously.

When Haley did not answer, Claudia whispered to Red, "How come she didn't answer me?"

Red whispered back, "She's like that when she's thinking really hard. My guess is she probably didn't even hear you. We could be a couple of giant toads right now and she wouldn't notice."

Claudia giggled. "What if we were giant cockroaches?"

"Nope," Red replied, "not even giant cockroaches."

Haley stopped at the edge of the slide area and sat down on a wooden beam that bordered the structure. She continued to rub her chin. Red and Claudia plopped down next to Haley.

Claudia leaned close to Red's ear. "Now what?" she asked in a loud whisper.

"We wait," Red explained.

There were not as many kids playing on the structure today. No one was going down the slide. Haley had hoped someone would go down so she could see if friction was still a problem. It did not look like anyone was going to use it anytime soon. Finally, she decided to go herself.

"Where are the climbers and sliders when you need them?" she murmured to herself.

The slide was over eight feet tall. She climbed the ladder and sat at the top. For a moment, she hesitated while trying to remember what normal speed had felt like the last time she went down the slide. When she felt like she was ready, she pushed off.

For the first couple of feet, it felt like the slide was going to work like normal. But, just as quickly, Haley felt herself slow and her pants bunch underneath her until she almost stopped. She had to grab at the sides of the slide and propel herself to keep moving. When she reached the bottom where it leveled, she stopped and did not go any farther.

It was still a problem. That much was clear. Haley hopped off the slide and whipped out her magnifying glass. She studied the surface of the slide, but it did not give her any more clues than it had the day before. She remembered her aunt had mentioned smooth surfaces could have as much or more friction than rough surfaces.

"Okay," she said to herself, "now let's see if the vegetable oil will make this work."

She decided to squeeze oil on the part of the slide where the friction seemed the worst. It was a good thing the top worked fine, because it was hard to reach anyway. Her plan was to climb up the slide part, not the ladder, squeeze on the oil, then use a paper towel to spread it around. She realized it was going to be hard to hold onto the slide with one hand and put the oil on with the other. She would need someone to steady her.

"Red," she called, "can you help me?"

Red stood, glanced at Claudia, raised her eyebrows, and shrugged her shoulders before walking over to Haley.

"I'm gonna climb up the slide, but I need you to hold onto me so I don't slip," Haley explained.

"What do you want me to hold onto?" asked Red.

"The back of my jeans," said Haley.

Red adjusted her glasses. "The back? So I'm going to be looking at your…" She frowned. "I always get the back. That's not your best side, you know."

"Please," Haley pleaded, "I'll make it up to you."

"Okay," she sighed. "It's a good thing we're best friends."

With Red close behind her, Haley started up the slide. Two feet from the top, Haley stopped and held on with one hand while pulling out the oil and paper towels with the other. Red grasped the belt loop on Haley's jeans and used her other hand to steady herself.

Haley used her teeth to pull the bottle's nozzle open. She squirted oil on the slide and used the paper towels to spread it around. They worked a section of the slide and then backed down a couple of feet before repeating the process. They hopped off when they reached the bottom and stood next to the slide to finish smearing oil on the level part.

They stood back to admire their work. It was hard to tell oil was on the slide, except it glistened a little more than the parts without oil. Haley and Red went back to where Claudia was sitting and put down the squeeze bottle and towels.

Claudia had observed the whole process. "I don't get it. What were you doing?"

Haley felt ready to try the slide again. She was excited at the thought of her experiment working. "I'm trying an experiment. The slide wasn't working right. It's not very slippery. You saw the first time I went down. I had to push myself down."

"Yeah, I saw," Claudia agreed. "It hardly worked at all."

"That's because there's too much friction. I don't know why it's acting like that. Friction is a really complex thing, but I bet the coefficient of friction for the slide is really big," Haley said in a knowing voice.

Claudia was clearly impressed. "Wow. How do you know so much about friction?" she asked.

Red piped up. "She's a scientist. That's why. She's got a lot of famous scientists in her family."

After Red's comments, Haley felt a little sheepish. She said, "Well, not everybody in my family is a scientist." She looked down. "But, I do want to be a scientist when I get older."

"What did you put on the slide to fix it?" inquired Claudia.

Haley held up the squeeze bottle. "Vegetable oil."

"Vegetable oil!" exclaimed Claudia. "Won't that get all over your clothes and stain?"

Haley's eyes widened. Claudia was right. She had not thought about that. She turned and stared at the slide.

The girls had not noticed that while they were talking, two first-grade boys had climbed the ladder and were preparing to go down. The first boy started down as though he *wanted* to go slowly. He had bent his knees and was using the flat underside of his tennis shoes as a brake to inch his way down the slide. He was almost at the point the oil started. The second boy was behind the first, also inching his way down.

Suddenly, Haley realized there were two problems. The first was the stain problem Claudia had mentioned. The second was more important. The oil was not a good idea if you *wanted* to go down the slide slowly.

She started toward the slide. She tried to yell "*Stop*", but the word stuck in her throat and would not come out. The scene unfolded before her eyes as though it were occurring in slow motion.

The first boy reached the oily section. Both of his feet flipped up into the air. He fell onto his back and his arms flailed wildly. A terrified look flashed across his face. He yelped as he accelerated down the slide and off the end of it, landing on his tailbone.

Seeing his playmate zip down the slide took the second boy by surprise. He panicked and lifted his feet just enough to slide into the oily section, where he too zipped to the bottom and off the end, landing on his friend. Both boys wailed in shock and pain.

Haley ran to the boys, followed by Red and Claudia. They tried to help the boys sit up.

Within seconds, a teacher arrived. He had the boys stay sitting and checked them for injuries. Although in pain, they did not seem seriously hurt. The boys' wails became whimpers as the shock wore off.

As the teacher helped the first boy to stand, he placed his hand on his back to steady him and asked, "What happened?"

Before Haley could answer, the teacher took his hand from the back of the boy's shirt and rubbed his fingers together. A puzzled look came over his face. He furrowed his eyebrows and sniffed at the oily substance on his fingers. The teacher ran his fingers along the surface of the slide and

rubbed them together again.

"There's oil on the slide," he exclaimed.

The teacher looked at the girls. "Do any of you know how oil got on the slide?"

Claudia's eyes widened. Red looked skyward and started to bite her lip. Haley grimaced. She tried to speak, but the best she could do was to squeak, "It's only vegetable oil."

The teacher stared at Haley. "Vegetable oil!" he said. "Why did you put oil on the slide?"

"It…uh…it was…uh…it was an experiment," Haley said weakly. She looked down at the squeeze bottle that was still in her hand.

The teacher reached out and took the squeeze bottle from Haley. "Girls," he said. "This isn't funny. We're going to take these boys to the nurse's office, and then we're all going to visit the principal."

The principal's office! It felt like a nightmare to Haley. She just wanted to make the slide better. How could everything go so wrong?

She hung her head in resignation as they walked to the building. Out of the corner of her eye, Haley could see Cynthia, Andrea, and Victoria standing to one side watching them. As she passed them, Haley could not help but notice the satisfied smirks on the faces of the CATT Club.

CHAPTER 9

The Principal's Office

The teacher escorted the three girls into the reception area just in front of the principal's office door and pointed them toward chairs across from the receptionist's desk. While the girls sat, the teacher knocked briefly on the principal's door and disappeared inside.

The receptionist gave Haley a kind smile before returning to her work. This was not Haley's first visit to the principal's office. She had been here two other times, but not recently.

Haley looked over at Red and Claudia. Red looked uncomfortable. She fidgeted and stared at the ceiling. Claudia sat with crossed arms and legs and a very worried look on her face.

Haley leaned forward in her chair with her elbows on her knees and cupped her chin in her hands. It was bad enough her experiment had not worked out as planned. And now they were in trouble for it. She wondered what she would say when they talked with the principal.

Should she lie and say she did not know how the oil got on the slide? That probably would not work since she had already told the teacher it was vegetable oil. Besides, she always felt guilty when she lied and was sure others could see it in her face.

Maybe she could say the boys should not have been on the slide anyway. The only problem was she could not think of a reason why. It was recess time and no one else was on the slide.

Before she could come up with any other ideas, the door to the principal's office opened. Both the teacher and the principal came out. The teacher left without another word. The principal motioned for the girls to come into his office. The girls' heads hung low as they filed in.

They sat in a row. Mr. Craft, the principal of Kinsley Bingham Elementary, closed his office door and sat on the corner of his desk facing the girls. Mr. Craft had short gray hair and a gray mustache. He was slim and much shorter than the teacher who had brought them here, although he seemed like a giant at this particular moment.

Haley gazed around the room. It looked the same as it had the last time she was here. The desk was a cluttered with a mound of papers. The other corner had a bookcase, but it did not hold many books. One shelf had several pictures, including one of the principal's wife, and one of his grown daughter with her husband and a small baby. There was also a picture of a cat with tiger stripes lying with a flower in its paws. Another shelf held a small golf trophy and a baseball on a small pedestal. Haley stared at the windows of his office wishing she could somehow make herself vanish and reappear outside.

Mr. Craft neither smiled nor frowned. In a soft voice, he simply asked, "Can someone tell me what happened?"

The girls remained silent. Claudia looked even more worried than before. Red adjusted her glasses and glanced at Haley. Haley bit her lip. Her shoulders felt heavy. Even after thinking about it, she was not sure what to say. But, she was sure she did not want Red and Claudia to get in trouble.

Finally, Haley stood. She stared at her shoes as she spoke. "Uh…Mr.

Craft. It's my fault. Really, it is. It wasn't Red or Claudia's idea. I was trying to fix the slide. It wasn't working right."

Haley explained that the slide was slow and her idea for solving the problem was to reduce the friction. She ended with, "I guess putting vegetable oil on it wasn't such a good idea, but it seemed like a good idea when I came up with it. I honestly wasn't trying to hurt anybody."

Mr. Craft took a deep breath and looked at Red and Claudia. "Is that right?" he asked.

They nodded.

"Fortunately, the boys were not hurt except for a couple of bumps," said Mr. Craft. He hesitated a moment. "Red and Claudia, you two can go to your classes. I need to talk with Haley privately for a couple more minutes."

The two girls got up. They both looked back at Haley before they left and closed door.

Mr. Craft moved around behind his desk and sat facing Haley. He picked up the plastic squeeze bottle which was lying on his desk and held it in his hands. "Haley, please sit down."

She sat on the edge of the chair and started to chew on her lower lip.

"I understand you didn't mean for something to go wrong," he said. "But this is—what—the second time in the past couple of years that you've ended up in my office?"

"Third," Haley replied.

"Ah. Third," Mr. Craft corrected himself. "In any case, you're now in fourth grade and need to show better judgment. I appreciate the fact that you took responsibility for the oil on the slide. I value your honesty on that."

A faint glimmer of hope shone through Haley's gloom.

Mr. Craft continued. "Your punishment…"

At hearing the word *punishment*, Haley's glimmer of hope flickered out like the flame of a candle blown out by a puff of wind.

"…needs to fit the actions. You will need to stay after school today and clean the oil off the slide completely. In addition, I'll also have to call your parents and talk with them."

Haley felt drained. Cleaning the slide did not feel too bad, but she dreaded the thought of what her parents would say when she got home.

With that, Mr. Craft dismissed Haley. She left his office, relieved to be finished with the conversation. The receptionist glanced up and gave her another kind look as she left.

After school, the same teacher who had discovered the oil on the slide also watched as Haley worked to clean it. The slide was much harder to clean than Haley thought it would be. Fortunately, Red and Claudia joined her to help. They carried two buckets to the slide. One held soapy water for cleaning and several rags. The other held only water, which they used to rinse the soap away. They had to make four trips to refill the buckets before the slide passed the teacher's inspection.

Once the slide was clean, they put away the buckets and rags and headed to the bicycle rack. "Hey, thanks for helping," Haley said. "I'd be there for another hour at least if it wasn't for you two."

Claudia spoke first. "Well, remember you rescued *me* this morning. I felt almost like the person being helped in the Good Samaritan parable. You did it even though you didn't really know me."

A tingling feeling went up Haley's spine. She turned to Claudia. "Have you been talking with my mom?" she asked as though expecting a secret conspiracy.

Claudia laughed. "How would I know your mom? You and Red are the first friends I've met since I started school three weeks ago."

Haley was still a bit suspicious. "Where did you learn the story about the Good Samaritan?"

Now it was Claudia's turn to stare. "C'mon, it's probably the most famous story in the Bible. Everybody must know that one. I must've learned that story at church when I was three or four years old. You've heard of it, right?"

"Yeah, I know that story," Haley said nonchalantly. She did not want Claudia to know about the conversation with her mother. She tried to sound convincing. "I guess I hadn't thought about it, but I suppose you're right that it worked out kinda like the story."

Claudia did not seem to notice. "Anyway, now we're friends. I'm glad I got the chance to help you a little. I think friends should help each other. It's too bad you got in trouble for your experiment."

"Oh, this one wasn't bad," Red said trying to be helpful. "Sometimes Haley's experiments are really exciting."

Haley frowned at Red.

Claudia suggested they could visit her grandmother's house on the weekend. "My grandmother could make lunch for all of us—real Mexican food!"

Haley and Red agreed enthusiastically. The girls got on their bicycles and rode together as far as the first intersection before splitting, and each heading home separately.

Sure enough, as promised, the principal, Mr. Craft, had called Mrs. Bellamy. Haley had barely arrived home, put her bicycle away, and walked into the house before Mrs. Bellamy intercepted her. The color of her face was slightly purple. She was definitely mad.

"Haley!" she shouted, "I got a telephone call from Mr. Craft at school. I want you in the living room on the sofa. Now! We need to have a talk!"

Haley did not waste any time. She scampered into the living room and planted herself on the sofa. Mrs. Bellamy followed and stood next to the sofa. From his sleeping spot at the other end, Einstein lifted his head to see what all the commotion was about. He looked at Haley, then at Mrs. Bellamy standing with her arms crossed. He quickly got up, jumped off the sofa, and trotted into the other room. Haley realized that although Einstein was old, he was still smart enough to clear out when Mrs. Bellamy was angry.

Mrs. Bellamy's voice was still loud. "Oil! You put oil on the slide at school! What in this world would make you think it's okay to put oil on the slide!"

Haley cringed. "It was only vegetable oil," she said. Her eyes began to well.

"Vegetable oil? Is that supposed to make me feel better?" asked Mrs. Bellamy. She started to pace back and forth. "The reason I'm only mad and not *really* mad is the fact you were honest with Mr. Craft and took responsibility."

A tear rolled down Haley's cheek. She did not say to her mother that *mad* and *really mad* seemed to be about the same.

"Red, Claudia, and I were trying an experiment to fix the slide," she whimpered.

Mrs. Bellamy stopped pacing. "What—an experiment? And who is Claudia?"

"She's the new girl," said Haley.

Mrs. Bellamy shook her head. "What new girl?"

Haley wiped her cheek with the back of her hand. Her hand felt wet from the tears. "The one I told you about that the CATT Club pushed around before. They did it again this morning, only Red and I made them stop."

A calmer look overtook Mrs. Bellamy. She sat on the other end of the sofa. She still looked mad, but clearly interested. "What do you mean *stopped*? How did you stop them?"

Haley told how she and Red confronted the CATT Club. She shared how afraid she felt, but knew she needed to do something. She also told more about Claudia, including the part about her parents being stationed overseas as diplomats while Claudia had to stay with her grandmother. When she was done, she clasped her hands in her lap, bit her lower lip, and waited.

A long silence ensued. Mrs. Bellamy breathed deeply. She pushed her hair back with both hands before she reached and pulled a small pillow from the sofa. She held it tight against her chest. Finally she spoke. "Haley, right now I'm not sure whether to hug you or be mad. I'm so pleased you helped Claudia and made a new friend in the process. You did the right thing. But I'm not happy about the oil on the slide. I think you have better judgment than that." She hesitated a few more seconds. "I think I need to let a day go by. I also need to talk to your dad. At a minimum, I think you'll need to go to bed right after dinner. We can talk more about this tomorrow."

Right after dinner, thought Haley. She usually got to stay up until nine on weekdays. That meant she'd be in bed before seven o'clock at the latest. She did not want to go to bed that early, but she knew that now was not the time to argue. "Okay," she said.

Shortly after dinner was finished and the kitchen cleaned up, Haley found herself in the upstairs bathroom preparing for bed. At the dinner table, they did not talk much about Haley's adventures at school. Haley was glad since, in particular, she did not want J.R. to know about the slide.

She had already bathed and changed into her flannel pajamas and was standing in front of the bathroom mirror while she brushed her teeth. She studied herself in the mirror. Her hair was slicked back and still wet from her bath, which made it appear much darker than normal. She leaned forward, close to the mirror, and saw her clear blue eyes staring back. She wondered if she really looked like a scientist. It doesn't matter what you look like, I suppose, anyone can be a scientist if they want to be one, she thought to herself.

From the mirror's reflection, she saw a movement behind her at the open bathroom door. At the same time, she heard J.R.'s voice singing, "Slip sliding away…slip sliding away ay ay …" As he sang, he flailed his head and arms as though he were a comedian pretending to be slipping on a grease patch.

Haley spun around. Her toothbrush still stuck out of her mouth. A few droplets of toothpaste flew from her mouth and splattered on the floor. Because of the toothpaste, she could not talk. "Grrrrrr," she growled as loud as she could.

Laughing wildly, J.R. jumped from the door, disappeared into his room, and shut his door with a bang.

Mr. Bellamy's voice came from downstairs. "I hope teeth are getting brushed up there," he called. "Also, you'd better be keeping the bathroom clean, since I cleaned it before dinner."

Haley turned back to the mirror. Why did J.R. have to be so mean sometimes? she wondered. She turned on the water and spit her toothpaste into the sink. She rinsed twice and patted her face dry with a hand towel.

The water in the sink drained very slowly. Haley watched the water gradually disappear down the drain. Over the last week, she noticed the problem getting worse. She tried pushing on the knob for the plug. It did not move; it was already in the open position.

The last time this happened, Mr. Bellamy took apart the U-shaped pipe underneath the sink and cleaned it. Haley remembered her father complaining that it looked like someone had stuck tissues and hair in the drain pipe.

Haley stared at the drain and absentmindedly started to rub her chin. Perhaps, she reasoned, if there were a way to unstick whatever was stuck in the pipe, her father would not have to take it apart again.

In her mind, she began to solve the problem. A wire stuck down the drain might work, but she knew it would be difficult for the wire to bend around the curve of the U-shaped pipe. She remembered advertisements on television for products that promised to unclog drains, but she was sure they did not have any of those. She tried taking out the drain plug to see if the clog was near the drain. She could not see anything.

"Hmm," she murmured to herself.

She rubbed her chin harder and scanned the bathroom. Her gaze lit upon the toilet plunger that was standing in the corner behind the toilet. She stopped rubbing her chin.

"That's it!" she exclaimed quietly.

She knew a plunger could create a lot of pressure in the drain pipe. So much so, that it could literally push the clog through with the force of water or air from the plunger. That is how it worked in the toilet. It should work the same in the sink.

Haley was excited to see if her idea would work. First, she filled the sink with more water so the level was high enough to cover the edges of the plunger. Then, she grabbed the plunger and placed it in the sink over the drain. She took a deep breath and pushed on the plunger with all of her strength.

SPLAT!

Water seemed to spray from nowhere straight at the mirror. Water splattered against it and went all over the bathroom. Haley let go of the plunger and stepped back in surprise.

"Awwwwk!" she squealed.

Haley slowly approached the sink. She did not understand what had happened. The water had seemed to spray from the edge of the sink closest to her. She carefully leaned over the sink and craned her head downward until it was almost upside down. Near the top of the sink, normally out of view, she saw the culprit—a small hole.

"Oh no," she groaned as she realized what had happened. The hole was another drain to keep the sink from overflowing. Since the hole was open, the plunger did not create pressure down to the U-shaped pipe. Instead, it pushed the water around the perimeter of the sink and out the other drain hole—straight at the mirror!

Haley looked up to see rivulets of water flowing down the mirror. Through the splattered mirror, she could see someone standing behind her in the doorway. It was too big to be J.R.

"What happened to the bathroom I just cleaned?" asked a man's voice.

Haley closed her eyes, turned around, and opened them again. She whispered, "Dad."

Mr. Bellamy stood in the doorway with a puzzled look on his face. He scratched his forehead and squinted. In a very slow, deliberate voice, he said, "There's a toilet plunger in the *sink*."

Haley did not dare move.

He raised both his eyebrows. The lines in his forehead became more pronounced. He repeated it again in the same slow deliberate voice. "There's a *toilet* plunger in the *sink*."

She tried to smile, but it felt more like a grimace, and shrugged her shoulders.

Still scratching his forehead, Mr. Bellamy turned away and slowly walked down the hall toward the stairs. He seemed to be talking to himself. "There's a *toilet* plunger in the *sink*."

After he left, Haley waited to see if he might turn around and come back. When it was clear that was not going to happen, she sprang into action. As quickly as she could, she put the plunger back next to the toilet. Next, she grabbed the towels on the rack and used them to wipe the mirror, counter, floor, and every other place she could find splattered water. From under the sink, she found cleanser and a pad and proceeded to scrub the sink until the pad was in tatters. From the hallway closet, she pulled a new set of towels and hung them in the bathroom.

When she was done, she raced to her bedroom, slipped into bed, and pulled the covers over her head. At this point, all Haley wanted to do was to hide in her bed and not move. It had been a very difficult day. For a long time, she lay awake with the events of the day repeating over and over in her mind. She felt good about her new friendship with Claudia, but she wondered why so much had gone wrong in the same day. Finally, she relaxed. Before she drifted to sleep, she remembered to say her prayers. "Dear God, thank you for my friends Claudia and Red. Please help me to have a better day tomorrow, Amen." Quickly, she was fast asleep.

∾ CHAPTER 10 ∾

The EZ Leaf Net Invention

The remaining days of the week were uneventful. Nevertheless, Haley was relieved when the weekend arrived. Saturday started out promising. It was a beautiful fall day. True, Haley could feel the bite of the first real frost, but the bright sun's rays were warm. Brown, orange, and rust leaves covered the ground like a colorful carpet. It was a good day to forget the troubles of the week.

The plan was to meet at Claudia's house a little before noon. Haley was glad to be going. After the principal's call to Mrs. Bellamy on Wednesday, Haley had been certain she would not be allowed to go anywhere for several days, if not weeks, or years.

However, much to Haley's surprise, her mother was very reflective when they talked the next day. Mrs. Bellamy made it clear that vegetable oil on the slide was not acceptable. But she liked Haley's honesty when facing the principal. In addition, she seemed glad that Haley helped Claudia. When Haley asked about going to Claudia's house, Mrs. Bellamy not only agreed, but also suggested Haley bring something to give to Claudia's grandmother.

Haley had the idea to make banana bread. She made two loaves in the morning and wrapped one to bring. She placed it carefully in her backpack. Since it was sunny, she wore her denim jacket. She carefully tucked her magnifying glass in her jacket pocket and buttoned it closed.

She hefted the backpack over her shoulder, buckled her helmet, and swung her leg over her bicycle. Quickly, she coasted down her driveway and headed in the direction of Claudia's house.

From her description, Haley knew where Claudia lived even though she had never been there before. It was along a route Haley sometimes took when she and Red were going to a pond they ice skated on in the winter. Her route also took her right past her school.

Haley rode slowly along the school perimeter farthest from the main building. From her vantage point, she could see workers on top of the building. She stopped briefly to watch.

Since the old school had not been upgraded, it needed lots of maintenance. Late each fall, workers readied the school for winter. They patched, cleaned, painted, and did whatever else the old building needed to make it through another year.

Haley watched them for a couple of minutes before continuing on her way.

As Haley neared Claudia's house, she could see Claudia in the front yard standing near some trees with a rake in one hand. She waved at Haley.

Haley slowed and jumped off her bike. "Hi Claudia," she said.

"I'm glad you could come," Claudia said. "I was worried you wouldn't be able to after getting in trouble."

"Me too. My mom was really mad at first. I thought I was gonna get grounded for at least a couple of years. She wasn't as mad the next day. I think it helped that I told the truth to Mr. Craft."

Haley looked around the yard. She noticed Claudia's grandmother's house was set back from the street. It was a small, pleasant-looking cottage. The outside was painted white. Both the trim and the front door were painted pale green. On either side of the front door were large windows. A pretty brick path led from the sidewalk straight to the front door.

The large yard made the house look even smaller. It almost seemed as if it were an island surrounded by a sea of grass. There were three trees in the front, but they were clustered on one side of the brick pathway. On the other side of the pathway and closer to the house was a badminton net ready for play.

Haley turned back to Claudia. "What cha' doing with the rake?"

Claudia looked at her rake, then up at the trees. The branches were completely bare. They had long since dropped their leaves. Even though the trees were in a small cluster, their leaves were widely scattered across the lawn. Her eyes brightened and she grinned at the obvious answer. "I'm raking leaves," she replied. "Do you want to help? There's another rake leaning against the side of the house."

"I guess that was kind of a dumb question. Sure, I'll help you," Haley said, feeling sheepish.

She pushed her bike to the side of the house and leaned it against the wall. She grabbed the rake, dropped her backpack and bike helmet near the front door, and quickly returned. She started raking near Claudia.

The girls talked as they raked. "My grandmother wanted me to rake all the leaves before you and Red arrived," said Claudia. "This is the first time I've ever raked leaves. I thought it would be pretty easy, but it's taking a lot longer than I thought."

"Really," Haley exclaimed. "You've never raked leaves?" She was surprised. It never occurred to her that someone might never have done it.

She asked, "How come?"

"I didn't need to," Claudia's replied. "I've only lived in San Francisco, Los Angeles, and Mexico City. The trees around there don't drop their leaves as much as they do here."

Haley remembered Claudia had mentioned San Francisco when they first met. "If your dad is an ambassador, why were you living in San Francisco and Los Angeles? Don't ambassadors have to live in Washington DC?"

Claudia explained, "He wasn't an ambassador then. Sometimes countries have consulates in other cities. My dad was working in the Los Angeles consulate when I was born. Then we moved to San Francisco." She stopped raking. "It's kinda funny to think my parents are diplomats for Mexico, but I've lived in the US more than I've lived in Mexico."

Haley stopped alongside her. "Yeah," she agreed. "That is kinda weird."

"And what's weirder is I'm still here in the US and my parents are in Chad." She suddenly looked sad and worried.

Haley noticed the change in Claudia's mood. "Are you okay?" she asked.

Claudia was silent for a few moments. It seemed as though she was trying to make up her mind about something. "I've been wondering something," she said finally. "I couldn't go with my parents to Chad because it's too dangerous for kids. But, if it's too dangerous for me, isn't it too dangerous for my parents? Shouldn't my parents not go if it's that dangerous? What do you think, Haley?"

Haley thought hard. She knew it must be difficult for Claudia to have her parents living overseas for two years. But, she had not considered the danger. She had to admit it did not make sense. "I see your point. But what can you do?"

Frustration crept into Claudia's voice. "There's nothing I can do," she said. "I just get to worry about them for two years." Claudia turned and began to rake again. "It's not fair," she added.

Haley tried to reassure Claudia. "I'm sure they'll be careful. I'm sure they'll be okay." Haley hoped she sounded convincing.

They were interrupted by the squeak of Red's bicycle brakes. "Sorry I'm late," Red said as she hopped off her bicycle. "My dad said I couldn't go anywhere until I cleaned my room. It was pretty much a disaster. Plus, I had to help my little brother with his room. Little brothers are such a pain."

Red had a younger brother who was four years old.

Haley smirked. "Older brothers can be a pain too," she said.

Red laid her bicycle down on the grass. "So, what'cha guys doing?" she asked.

Haley and Claudia were standing next to each other holding rakes. Haley remembered Claudia's reaction when she asked that same question earlier.

Haley and Claudia stared at Red with a deadpan look on their faces. At the same time, they turned their heads to each other and gave an amused look. In unison, they looked up at the bare branches and then back to Red.

Red adjusted her glasses and played along. "Oh," she said. "Dumb question, I guess, since you're holding rakes."

At that all three girls burst into laughter.

"You could help," Claudia offered, "but, we've only got two rakes. We could take turns."

Haley looked around the yard. Despite hers and Claudia's raking, only a small part of the yard was clear. Their pile of raked leaves was small.

"This yard is too big," she complained, "Even if we had another rake, it would still take forever. There's gotta be a faster way."

She scanned the yard. Her eyes lit upon the badminton net. She began to rub her chin.

Claudia said, "I don't think my grandmother has anything else we could use…"

Haley did not hear her. She dropped her rake and went to the net. She walked around it and thought furiously.

The net was low enough that Haley could reach it easily. The two poles that held the net were about ten feet apart. String ran from the poles to stakes in the ground. A picture formed in Haley's mind.

The girls were still standing near the trees when Haley turned to them. "I have an idea," she called.

Red and Claudia came to the badminton net. "What's your idea?" Red asked. "I hope it doesn't have anything to do with vegetable oil."

"No, no, no," Haley said. Her voice filled with excitement. She spoke rapidly, "We can use this badminton net to scoop leaves much faster than using rakes."

Claudia looked skeptical. "I don't think I understand."

"Don't you see," Haley explained patiently, "we take the string off and hold the poles so the net is upside down. We drag it along the grass just like fishermen sometimes drag their nets along the bottom of the ocean. The net will scoop leaves much faster than we can with just rakes."

Red understood immediately. She nodded vigorously. "That's a great idea. I bet we could get the yard clear in, like, five or ten minutes. Let's do it."

That was all the prompting that was needed. The girls unhooked the strings from the poles and flipped the net down.

With Haley directing, Claudia held one pole while Red held the other.

They kept the edge of the netting against the grass and pulled the poles.

It worked just as Haley had envisioned. Few leaves were left behind as they dragged the net. Working from the farthest parts of the lawn, they moved leaves to a pile near the trees. In less than ten minutes, the yard was clear of leaves. All that remained was the pile. They put the badminton net back where they had found it.

The three girls stood back to admire their handiwork.

Red was impressed with how quickly they had cleared the lawn. "What a great idea!" she exclaimed. "I bet you could sell your invention for lots of money."

"Wow! You really are a good inventor," Claudia chimed in. "You could call it the EZ Leaf Net."

Haley was also pleased with how well her idea worked, but said modestly, "It did work pretty well. Didn't it?"

They were so absorbed in admiring the neat pile of leaves that they did not see the fast-approaching bicycles.

Red was the first to notice. "Look out!" she cried. She jumped back and pulled at Haley and Claudia.

Zoom!

The first bicyclist missed the girls by inches and plowed straight through the leaf pile. A second bicyclist zoomed through the pile, and then a third. Leaves scattered in all directions. The first bicyclist turned and headed back in the direction of the girls.

It was the CATT Club!

Haley, Red, and Claudia took cover behind one of the trees, trying to keep the trunk between them and the marauding CATT Club.

Cynthia rode back through the leaf pile. As she went through it, she used her feet to kick at the pile and scatter the leaves even more. Andrea and Victoria did the same. The CATT Club circled again and stopped.

"What are you doing!" Red cried angrily. She started toward the CATT Club. Haley and Claudia quickly pulled her back.

"We don't need to get mad," Haley whispered urgently to Red.

"Too late. I'm mad," Red declared. She tugged against Haley and Claudia's hands.

Cynthia straddled her bicycle and folded her arms across her chest. Her dark brown eyes looked even darker and meaner than usual. "Oh, *sorry*," she said sarcastically. "We didn't mean to mess up your hard work. It was an accident. We'll try to get out of your way."

"Like it was an accident. They almost ran us over," Red muttered.

"It doesn't matter," Claudia said in a low soothing voice. "Let it go. It's not worth it. Besides, we've got something they don't know about."

Haley knew at once what Claudia was talking about. "That's right!" she murmured.

Red turned her head toward Claudia. "Huh?" she said. She still did not understand.

The CATT Club started at them one more time. Haley, Red, and Claudia stayed behind the tree trunk as the CATT Club zoomed through the leaf pile again. By this time, there was not much of a pile. Victoria stopped briefly in the middle of where the pile had been. She narrowed her eyes and squinted through her glasses at the girls. She yelled, "We told you not to make an enemy of the CATT Club!" She pushed off and pedaled after Cynthia and Andrea.

~ CHAPTER 11 ~

Mexican Hot Dogs

After the CATT Club left, the girls came out from behind the tree. They surveyed the scene. Red spoke first. "What were you two talking about?" she was still mad. "They messed up all our work. What do you mean we have something they don't know about? It was like you were talking in code."

"I was talking in code, sort of, in case they could hear us," said Claudia. "I didn't want them to know how easy it'd be to clean up the lawn again. Remember, we have Haley's new EZ Leaf Net invention!"

A look of understanding dawned across Red's face. She sucked in her breath sharply. "You're right! I forgot," she said. "We can scoop these leaves back in a pile in nothing flat."

The girls raced to the badminton net. Within minutes, all the leaves scattered by the CATT Club were back in a tidy pile next to the tree, and the net was back in its place.

Haley was pleased. Not only had her invention worked twice, but it also allowed the girls to avoid a confrontation with the CATT Club.

"Now that we have the leaves back in a pile, what do we do with them?" Red asked.

"My grandmother told me she wanted me to put the leaves in some bags," Claudia said. "Wait here and I'll see if I can find them." She disappeared inside the house.

All the excitement and work made Haley feel hot and tired. She took off her denim jacket, sat down on the ground next to the leaf pile, and leaned against the tree. Red plopped on the grass and sat cross-legged facing Haley.

"I'm hungry," Red declared.

Haley did not hear her. She was looking at the leaves next to her. She reached out with her hand and plucked a bright orange leaf from the pile and held it by the stem. Slowly, she rotated the leaf with her fingers and began to study every detail. It was a maple leaf. The main part of the leaf expanded out from the stem in a wide pattern. It curved until it reached a point, similar to the point of a crescent moon, before dipping and curving upward again into another point. The surface was dry and stiff. Haley knew if she closed her fingers around the leaf, it would crush into small pieces. She marveled that a leaf would transform itself from green and pliable to orange and stiff so quickly.

Red could see Haley was absorbed with the leaf. She sighed and waited patiently.

Haley reached for her denim jacket, unbuttoned the pocket with her magnifying glass, and pulled it out.

She rolled over onto her elbows and knees and leaned her shoulder against the tree. Carefully, she placed the leaf on the grass and reached for more leaves to create a small pile. With her magnifying glass, Haley studied them closely. She could see the different colors, details of the veins, and even how the surface varied from leaf to leaf.

Haley could also see bright spots on the leaves from where the sun shone through the magnifying glass. Depending on how she held it, the spots varied from wide and circular, to small pinpoints.

"Ahem." It was Red clearing her throat.

Haley craned her neck and looked up. Claudia had returned with lawn bags under one arm. She and Red were standing over her looking down. A tinge of embarrassment swept her face. She had not noticed them.

"C'mon Haley," said Red. She motioned with her arm. "Let's finish up the leaves so we can eat lunch. I get cranky when I get too hungry."

Red was right in more ways than one. Although she had not noticed it before, Haley realized her own stomach was rumbling. And Red did tend to get somewhat crabby when she was hungry.

"Sorry," she said. "I was just checking out the different kinds of leaves. Have you ever wondered why some leaves turn brown while others turn yellow or orange?"

"Actually, no," Red stated flatly. "Although I've been wondering what Mexican lunch food tastes like."

It looked like Red had reached her crabby point. Haley knew the best solution was to get her fed fast.

Haley carefully propped her magnifying glass against the tree next to her small pile of leaves. She planned to study the leaves again later. "I want to keep my little pile of leaves, because I'm not done studying them. We can put the others in the bags."

Claudia assured her. "We'll start from the other side of the big pile so we won't accidentally take your pile."

Red was getting more agitated. "Can we get started now before I fall over from hunger?"

Claudia looked taken aback.

Haley reassured her. "Don't worry," she said, "Just like she said, Red does get crabby when she's hungry. Perfectly normal for her."

Claudia held the bag open while Haley and Red used their hands to stuff leaves into it. They quickly filled it. Filling the first bag had only made a small dent in the pile. She held open the second bag.

"It's going to take forever. At this rate, we'll starve to death before we finish," Red grumbled.

Just then, Claudia's grandmother came out onto the porch. She called out to the girls. "You must be hungry. Why don't you girls stop and come inside for lunch." She went back inside the house.

The girls dropped the bag and started toward the house.

"Whew!" Red sighed, "Just in time! I can't wait to try real Mexican food."

Claudia grinned. "Don't worry. We'll feed you first."

"What kind of Mexican food did your grandmother fix us?" Haley asked.

"I don't know," Claudia replied, "but it's always great. She's a terrific cook."

The girls entered the house. It was as small and tidy on the inside as it looked on the outside. The front door opened into the living room. Directly behind the living room was an open kitchen on one side and a dining area on the other. At the back of the house, two doors led to each of the two small bedrooms.

Claudia's grandmother greeted them warmly. "You must be Haley," she said as she extended her hand for Haley to shake. She had an accent similar to Claudia's, only slightly stronger. "Claudia told me you are quite a talented scientist and inventor." She seemed so genuine that Haley immediately felt at ease.

Claudia's grandmother was tiny. Haley was about average height for a 10-year old girl, but could see she was already taller than Claudia's grandmother. Haley could also see the clear resemblance between her and Claudia. She had reading glasses perched on her nose.

"You must be Red." She held out her hand toward Red. "Claudia mentioned your beautiful hair."

Red blushed and adjusted her glasses as she shook her hand. Usually kids at school used other words to describe Red's hair. Haley could tell she was pleased to hear the word *beautiful.*

"It's nice to meet you both. Claudia has told me how glad she is to have you as best friends."

Now it was Claudia's turn to blush.

"It's nice to meet you too, Mrs. Valencia," Haley said in a formal manner, and extended her hand.

Claudia's grandmother smiled broadly. "Oh, please don't call me Mrs. Valencia. I feel old enough when Claudia calls me Grandma, but she has to call me that. You two can call me Alice."

Alice? Haley thought. Almost all the grown-ups she knew were called by their last name, plus mister or miss, except Aunt Gabby of course.

Alice's voice interrupted her thoughts. "I know you girls are hungry, so why don't you clean up while I put your lunch on your plates."

The girls quickly washed and sat at the dining table. Red was almost beside herself. "I can't wait to try real Mexican food."

Alice came from the kitchen balancing three plates. She placed one in front of each girl. Haley stared at the food on the plate. She was not sure what real Mexican food was supposed to look like. She eyed it suspiciously. It did not look like Mexican food to her. In fact, it looked remarkably similar to—

"I didn't know hot dogs were Mexican food," Red blurted out.

"Who told you we were having Mexican food?" Alice asked.

Claudia suddenly looked very small in her chair. She raised her hand. "Me," she said in a quiet voice. "I thought you were going to cook traditional food."

Alice finally understood. "Ah. I see. I'm sorry, Claudia, but I didn't realize I was supposed to make something else for your friends. I figured I would just make something everyone would like." She clapped her hands together. "Next time I'll make enchiladas and tamales. But today, we're having…Mexican Hot Dogs!"

The girls looked at each other. They were not sure what she was talking about.

She disappeared into the kitchen and reappeared in seconds holding a jar of salsa. "Here," she said. "Spoon some of this on your hot dogs to make genuine Mexican hot dogs!"

The girls laughed. Haley dipped a spoon into the jar and spread salsa the length of her bun. She tried a bite. It was pretty good! After Haley, Red and Claudia added salsa to their dogs. Haley watched in amazement as Red ate three hot dogs. Haley and Claudia ate two each. The girls lounged in their chairs, their stomachs full.

It was Claudia who noticed it first.

"Does it smell like something is burning?" she asked.

Red sniffed the air. "It smells like burning leaves to me," she said.

It smelled like burning leaves to Haley too. Haley thought it unusual. Many people bagged their leaves instead of burning them. Plus it was getting far enough along in the season that most people were done with their leaf raking.

Alice came from the kitchen. She also sniffed the air. "It does smell like burning leaves, although I wonder who?" she said.

She frowned and made her way to one of the front living room windows. As she approached the window, she commented, "I see smoke drifting this way."

She reached the window and stood staring out for a few seconds. Then she quickly turned and reached for a telephone sitting on a side table next to the sofa. She calmly said, "Girls, stay in the house. There's a fire in the front yard. I'm going to call the fire department."

The girls rushed to the window and looked out. They could see flames jumping up from where the leaf pile had been. The flames had scorched the tree trunks and set the lower branches on fire.

After Alice hung up the phone, she and the girls went out onto the front porch and waited.

Within two minutes they could hear the wail of a siren approaching. A fire truck drew up to the curb. Out jumped two firefighters who quickly went to work. They connected a hose to the truck and sprayed water where the leaves had been, and then started spraying up into the trees. Soon the fire was out. All that was left of the leaf pile was a sopping wet mess of ash. The tree trunks and lower branches had black scorch marks.

Haley could see the two firefighters poking around the ash pile. One firefighter was tall and beefy. The other was shorter and wiry. She recognized them both. They were the same firefighters who had come to her house after the refrigerator explosion.

The beefy firefighter stooped down at the base of the tree trunk and picked something up. He held whatever it was in his hand as he made his way to where Alice and the girls waited. He recognized Haley and winked at her.

Alice greeted him. "Thank you so much for coming quickly. I can't imagine how the leaves caught on fire."

"I think I have an idea how it started," said the beefy firefighter. He held up something that glinted in the sunlight. "It looks like the fire started near the tree trunk. I found this propped up against the trunk," he said. "My guess is the sun caught the magnifying glass at the right angle and focused the sun into a hot point on some of the leaves. Once it started burning, it spread to the rest. I don't see anything else that could have started it."

Haley suddenly felt very small. Her heart sank.

"Hey, that's Haley's magnifying glass," Red said helpfully.

"Haley's?" the beefy firefighter exclaimed. "Are you sure?" he asked. The firefighter raised the magnifying glass to his face and peered at it closely. "It looks like something's engraved on the handle," he said. He read the inscription out loud. "It's says *To Haley, Love Grandpa*." He looked up.

Everyone turned and stared at her.

Haley stood rock still. Her face was expressionless. Her mouth hung half open. Her shoulders slumped. She was not sure what she should say.

Seconds ticked away in silence.

How could this happen on a day that started so well? Sunshine, her new EZ Leaf Net invention, outsmarting the CATT Club, being with her best friends, meeting Claudia's grandmother, Mexican hot dogs—so many reasons to feel happy. Now this!

She was sure Claudia's grandmother would never want her to come to their house again. Haley felt especially sad Claudia might not be her friend anymore.

Her thoughts were broken by the voice of the firefighter. "Here," he said gently, holding out her magnifying glass to her. She slowly took it from his hand. The heat, flames, and ash of the fire had tarnished and scorched its brass surface. It was no longer so shiny. She jammed the magnifying glass into her jeans pocket.

The firefighter added, "I think this might be yours too. Sorry Haley." He held out Haley's denim jacket. It was still dripping. It had gotten wet when the firefighters sprayed the fire with water. The wrist of one sleeve looked slightly singed. It was an expensive jacket. Haley's mother was not going to be happy.

The firefighter turned and went back to the fire truck.

Haley could feel her eyes beginning to well with tears. She blinked several times. She did not want to cry, but started to cry anyway. She had trouble seeing through her tears. She did not want anyone to say anything. She just wanted to go home, alone.

Haley felt someone near her. It was Claudia. She quietly said, "It's okay, Haley. It's not your fault."

Haley felt someone hug her. It was Alice. Her voice was soothing. "It was an accident," she said in a kind tone. "It's not your fault. Try not to feel bad. Things happen. Sometimes we're blessed with good things. Sometimes something goes wrong, but good still comes from it." Alice looked straight at Haley. "I'm not upset," she said. "I'm still glad you came. I'm still glad you're Claudia's friend."

Haley felt relieved. The weight on her shoulders seemed to lift. She could not believe it. Claudia was still her friend! Alice still liked her! She began to feel better.

Red piped up. "I can think of one good thing about the fire," she said brightly.

"What's that?" Haley asked.

"We don't have to bag all the leaves," Red exclaimed. "They're already gone!"

They all laughed at that.

Haley looked down the steps and spied her book bag.

"I almost forgot!" she cried.

Alice, Claudia, and Red watched as she scampered down the stairs and ran back up with her book bag.

"I almost forgot," Haley repeated as she dug deep into her bag and

pulled out the loaf of banana bread. She held it out to Alice. "Here," she said breathlessly. "I made this for you this morning. I meant to give it to you when I arrived."

Alice took it carefully from her hands. "That is very thoughtful, thank you so much," she said.

She laughed, "Since you girls saved all that time by not bagging the leaves, should we all go inside and have banana bread for dessert? How about if we spice it up with some Mexican Hot Chocolate!"

CHAPTER 12

The Less Than Perfect Scientist

Haley waited patiently for her Sunday school class to start. As usual, her mother made sure the Bellamy's were at least ten minutes early to church. Haley was certain her mother's focus on punctuality was somehow related to her profession as an accountant. She knew two things about her mother: one, she would not allow money to be spent unnecessarily and, two, they would always arrive on time for any event. In some ways, Haley preferred her father's approach. He was comfortable arriving in the nick of time, or even five minutes late.

The church Haley and her family attended was fairly new, at least by Ann Arbor standards. Regardless of denomination, most churches in the city could trace their history by decades, if not by a century or more in some cases. The Bellamy's church was twelve years old, only two years older than Haley herself. In addition to the main sanctuary, it had a second building that housed a basketball court and several classrooms. It was in one of these that Haley waited.

Haley liked Sunday school well enough, although often it reminded her of regular school. There were usually eleven or twelve kids in the class. The children sat around the perimeter of a large table so everyone faced inward and could see everyone else. Although they sometimes did a craft or other activity, most Sundays were spent in discussion after reading a section in the Bible.

In some ways, Haley liked Sunday school better than regular school. There was never any homework, she could choose to participate in the discussion a lot or a little depending on how she felt, and there was no one mean like the members of the CATT Club.

The girls outnumbered the boys in the class by two to one, which was fine by Haley. When there were too many boys, they could be loud and disruptive, which was especially annoying when Haley was in the middle of daydreaming about a new idea or invention. At the moment Haley was using her early arrival as another daydreaming opportunity.

She rested her elbows on the table and cradled her chin in her hands. A glazed look came over her face as her mind wandered to the impending winter. A picture of the pond near the school entered her mind. Haley and Red called it a pond, but it could be considered a small lake. It was the pond Haley and Red went ice skating on after it was frozen.

She remembered watching windsurfers on some of the larger lakes in the summer. It sure would be neat, she thought, to do something like that, but on the ice. Haley wondered if she could make a contraption.

She was just beginning to come up with some ideas when someone bumped her arm, jostling her out of her daydream. Her chin dropped out of her cupped hands and almost hit the table. She felt another nudge at her arm and heard someone say, "Haley, are you awake?"

Her eyes were still blurry from her daydream. She tried to focus them on the offender. When her vision cleared, it was Claudia much to her surprise.

Haley was confused. "What're you doing here?" she asked.

Claudia grinned. "I'm here for church of course, same as you."

"But you don't go to my church," Haley replied. She still felt confused. "Your grandmother doesn't either. At least, I've never seen her here."

"Well, you're right. My grandmother belongs to another church," Claudia explained. "I've been going to her church with her for the last couple of weeks since I arrived. The problem is everybody there is my grandmother's age and older. There's hardly any kids at all. I told my grandmother that it wasn't very much fun for me. She said we could try some other churches that had more kids and see if maybe we could find a church that would work for both of us. I didn't know you went here. This is the first one we tried. Pretty lucky, huh! I said *Hi* when I came in the room, but you didn't even see me. You looked like you sometimes do when you're thinking hard. I thought maybe you weren't glad to see me."

At Claudia's words, Haley was suddenly worried. Had she been that rude? She was happy to see Claudia. She didn't want her to think otherwise. Especially after how nicely Claudia and Alice had treated her after the fire. "Uh, yes, I mean no," she stammered. "I mean, yes, I'm glad you're here. I just didn't expect to see you—"

She started to feel embarrassed until she saw Claudia's face and realized Claudia had been joking with her. "You're giving me a hard time for being zoned out, aren't you?" she asked. Now it was her turn to laugh.

Before Haley and Claudia could talk further, Mrs. Klein called the class to order. "Okay, let's get started. We'll open in prayer in a minute, but first I want to tell you about the lesson. Today we're going to discuss a passage from the book of Luke. I think you'll recognize it, or maybe have studied it before, but we're going to look at it from a different angle than what you're accustomed to." She followed with a question, "How many of you have heard of, or read, the Parable of the Good Samaritan?"[4]

4. Luke 10:25

Haley's heart jumped a bit. With all that had gone on in the last week, it almost seemed weird that they would be talking about the Good Samaritan. She knew she would want to pay attention and contribute to today's discussion!

Haley turned to Claudia to see what she might be thinking. Claudia grinned back at her and winked.

That afternoon, Haley was sitting cross-legged on her living room sofa. Einstein was curled in a ball on her lap, effectively trapping her. That is, until he moved to his next sleeping spot. Haley held a mug of hot chocolate, which she carefully rested on Einstein. He did not seem to mind the warm cup on his back.

Aunt Gabby sat across from Haley in one of the two overstuffed living room chairs. Her feet were tucked underneath her. She held a mug of coffee close to her face and breathed in the steam. Today her hair was purple, and she wore contact lenses that made her eyes a very pretty shade of violet.

It was somewhat unusual for Aunt Gabby to visit on the weekend. Her usual days for visits were Tuesdays. However, she explained she was going to be gone all week on a business trip to Livermore, California, and did not want go an extra week without seeing the Bellamy clan.

Haley considered the prior week. As best as she could tell, she conducted two experiments and created one invention. The exploding root beer bottle and oil on the slide were both failed experiments. She was sure about that. The EZ Leaf Net invention was definitely a success. It was unclear how she should view the fire started by her magnifying glass. She was not conducting an experiment at the time, but she had been studying the leaves. If she were to classify it, she was pretty sure it would fall in the failure category.

She felt a small pang of despair.

Aunt Gabby leaned forward. "What'cha thinking, Haley? You've got the same look I've seen on Einstein when he's done something bad," she said. Her violet eyes danced. "The only differences between you and him are your ears are smaller and you don't have a tail to tuck between your legs."

Haley hesitated a moment. She knew her aunt would understand, but she was not sure whether she wanted to talk about it right then.

Aunt Gabby tried humor again. "C'mon Haley, what's on your mind? I'll give you one of Einstein's kibbles."

Haley made a face. "Yuck," she said. She sighed heavily. "Of course, maybe I should eat *dog food* as much as I've been in the *dog house* this week."

Nodding, Aunt Gabby said, "I thought you might be thinking too much about this week." She leaned back in her chair, took a sip from her mug, and looked squarely at Haley. "You're probably even thinking about the fire that scorched your jacket sleeve," she said steadily.

An electric shock went through Haley's body. How did Aunt Gabby know about that? Haley had not told anyone. Alice had helped her dry her coat and cleaned the sleeve so that the singe mark was barely visible. Her parents had not even noticed.

"How did you know?" she said breathlessly.

Aunt Gabby winked. "An eye for small details I guess," she said. "What happened?"

Haley told the story of helping Claudia to clear leaves from the yard. She included the details of the EZ Leaf Net invention, the CATT Club, Mexican hot dogs, and the fire. She ended with, "Alice didn't call my parents or anything. She said since she wasn't upset, there wasn't any need to talk with them about it. In fact, Alice and Claudia met Mom and Dad after the church service. Neither one said anything about the fire or my jacket. How'd you know?"

"I was partially guessing, at least on the fire part," she said. Aunt Gabby looked satisfied with herself. "You're right though. The burn mark on your sleeve isn't really noticeable to most people." She paused several seconds. "Unless, of course, someone did almost exactly the same thing in the past."

At that moment, Mr. Bellamy strode into the living room. "Unless someone did what in the past?" he asked. He plopped himself down on the sofa opposite from Haley. As he did, he held his steaming mug away from himself in the event the waves inside the cup should spill the hot liquid over the sides.

Haley did not say anything.

Einstein lifted his head. His body slowly rose. He stepped from Haley's lap and moved across the sofa to Mr. Bellamy while giving two tired wags with his tail. Einstein climbed into Mr. Bellamy's lap and circled three times before lying down. Mr. Bellamy reached down and scratched Einstein behind the ears.

"It must be nice to be a dog," he said. "Eat. Sleep. Eat. Sleep. Occasionally wag your tail." He shrugged and gestured at no one in particular. "So what were you two talking about, someone doing something in the past?"

Haley remained silent.

Aunt Gabby rescued her. "We were talking about trying different experiments and how it doesn't always work like you think it should. For example, Haley's root beer experiment and the oil on the slide turned out differently." She conveniently neglected to mention Haley's fire. "I was just telling her that I've had a few experiments that didn't work out as planned."

Mr. Bellamy let loose a loud snort, "Ha! A *few* that didn't work out. I seem to remember more than just a few when we were younger. Did you tell Haley about the car windshield?"

Haley looked at Aunt Gabby with a start. "What windshield?" she asked.

A red tinge spread across Aunt Gabby's cheeks. It was a few moments before Haley realized her aunt was embarrassed. As long as Haley could remember, her aunt seemed to relish the attention her hair, eyes, and sometimes outrageous behavior seemed to garner. Haley was very curious about what could cause her aunt such feelings of embarrassment.

"Oh," she said with a wave of her hand, "I managed to break the windshield on Dad's car. That's all."

"That's all. Yeah right," Mr. Bellamy chortled. "It not just that she broke the windshield, but how she broke it, and what your grandpa did to her afterward."

Now Aunt Gabby's cheeks were flaming red. "You're getting back at me for the raisins and pickles on the pizza, aren't you?" She directed her question at Mr. Bellamy.

Curiosity was killing Haley. "How did you break the windshield?" she asked impatiently.

Aunt Gabby sighed again before answering. "I was thirteen years old at the time. Our dad, your grandpa, wanted me to scrape the ice off of the windows of his car. Well, scraping a frozen window in the winter is, as you know, hard, and it takes forever. I got the idea that maybe I could use hot water and pour it on the window to make the ice melt. I knew it'd be a lot faster and easier than scraping. Anyway, I heated up some water. Actually, I heated it up a lot and poured it on the windshield. It definitely cleared the ice, but the fast temperature change on the windshield made it crack. The windshield looked like a big spider web with crack lines all over it. Dad was not happy."

Mr. Bellamy piped up, "You left out the best part."

Haley had not thought Aunt Gabby's cheeks could get any redder, but they did. "What's the best part?" she asked.

Silence ensued for almost a minute before Aunt Gabby answered. "My dad spanked me. Here I am, thirteen years old, and he spanks me for breaking the windshield. I hadn't been spanked since I was, what, five years old. He puts me over his knee like I'm five again and paddles my bottom."

Mr. Bellamy broke in, laughing as he spoke, "And as he spanks her, he's saying, 'This way you'll remember that materials with low conductivity are susceptible to thermal shock from rapid temperature changes.' He's giving her a science lesson while he's spanking her! It was hilarious."

Aunt Gabby stuck out her tongue at Haley's father. "Not so funny when you're the one over the knee," she retorted. She looked thoughtful for a moment. "On the other hand, I never forgot that."

"Wow, Aunt Gabby. I didn't know some of your ideas didn't work out." Haley was intrigued. She had assumed that since her aunt was a great scientist, all of her experiments must work the first time.

"Oh, I can't tell you how many times my experiments didn't work," she explained. "I remember when I was in college. One of my first laser experiments didn't go so well. I used the wrong barrier material and burned a hole right through it, not to mention the wall behind it. My professor got a bit irritated at that."

Mr. Bellamy motioned at Haley. "Come over here and sit next to me," he said.

Haley scooted across the sofa. Mr. Bellamy put his arm around her and gave her a hug. "Honey, granted I'm not as interested in science as my dad, or as my famous sister here. But I deeply care about you and

want to encourage you to pursue your dreams. You know, in many ways you're a lot like your Aunt Gabby. She always was thinking about experiments and inventions when we were growing up. Look at her now. She's a physicist and loves what she does. Like her, you're blessed with tremendous talent and lots of brains. Sometimes I'm less enthusiastic—the exploding refrigerator comes to mind—but for the most part, I'm glad you love science and I want to encourage you to follow your dreams."

Haley snuggled closer to her father. At that moment, she felt loved and very secure.

"After all," her father concluded, "you're my girl of sparks and shooting stars!"

∽ CHAPTER 13 ∽

Suspended!

Over the next several days the temperature dropped steadily. Although snow had not yet arrived, winter was definitely near. Haley found her denim coat was woefully inadequate, so she began wearing both a sweater and heavier jacket. She rode her bike to school but needed to wear wool gloves so her fingers would not turn bright red as they became numb from the cold. She would not be able to ride to school much longer, and would need to start walking instead.

It was Wednesday and Haley was already looking forward to the upcoming weekend. Mostly, she just wanted to get through the week without another mishap. She had been looking at each uneventful day as an accomplishment.

Haley successfully navigated the morning without any problems. She knew it must be close to lunchtime because her stomach growled. She had only lunch and a couple more hours before she could chalk up another successful day.

Mrs. Vasey stood at the front of the classroom. She was reviewing how to approach and solve word problems using multiplication and division. Outside of science, Haley's next most favorite subject was math. Haley liked math because she was good at it, and also because she could use it to solve problems.

At the moment, it was a bit hard to concentrate on Mrs. Vasey because Red was passing notes to her. Normally she was more than willing to pass notes, but she did not like doing so in the middle of her favorite subject. However, Red was her best friend, and she felt obligated to read each note and send a reply.

The current note read, *Cage West keeps staring at you. Do you think he likes you?*

Cage West was a boy who sat on the other side of the room. He had long dark hair that always seemed to be falling over the front of his face. He also wore a T-shirt without any sleeves no matter the weather. This was the first year Haley had a class with Cage in it. He had not said more than two words to her since the beginning of the school year, so Haley could not think of any reason why he might like her.

She wrote a reply note, *I don't care if he likes me. Besides he probably can't even see me with his hair over his eyes.* She passed the note to Red and watched her face as she read it.

Red did her best to stifle a giggle. She began to scribble another note. Haley knew it was longer because it was taking a lot of time to finish it. She passed the note to Haley.

Haley opened the new note and started to read it. She was about half-way through it before she became aware that Mrs. Vasey had stopped talking. Haley looked up from the note.

Mrs. Vasey was at the entrance to the classroom talking in quiet tones to someone. It was the same teacher who took Haley to the principal's office after the oil-on-the-slide episode. They looked in her direction several times. An eerie sensation climbed Haley's spine. She had the feeling they were talking about her.

"Haley, would you please come here," Mrs. Vasey called in a low voice.

Haley could feel all eyes on her as she made her way to the door. Haley wondered if she was in trouble for passing notes. It did not seem likely. Usually, Mrs. Vasey would simply pluck the note from the offender and take away one behavior point. No behavior points had been taken from Haley all week. She had been extra careful to avoid trouble.

She looked back at Red. Red pushed her glasses on her nose and made an expression that clearly indicated she did not understand what was going on.

When Haley reached the door, Mrs. Vasey leaned over and whispered to her, "Haley, please go with this teacher. He's going to take you to the principal's office. Mr. Craft would like to speak with you."

As Haley walked with the teacher, her mind raced. Why would the principal need to see her? What did he want to talk about? Was she in trouble? Had her parents been in a car wreck?

Mr. Craft was waiting for Haley when she arrived at his office. He had a grim look on his face as he promptly ushered her into his office.

While Haley sat in a chair in front of the desk, Mr. Craft went around and sat on the other side so the desk was between them. Haley noticed the desk was unusually clear of clutter. The smooth expanse of the desk seemed like a vast ocean between them. This was not going to be a friendly conversation.

Mr. Craft gazed at Haley but did not say anything immediately. He reached into his desk, pulled out an item, and placed it in the middle of his desk before returning to his gaze to her.

It was a small plastic bottle. Haley was confused. Why would Mr. Craft summon her to his office only to give her a plastic bottle? She looked at it more closely.

Then it hit her, it was almost the same kind of plastic squeeze bottle she used for the oil she put on the slide. It might even be the same bottle.

It did not make sense though. They had already talked about the slide. Haley had cleaned it. Mr. Craft had spoken with Haley's mother. She had thought it was all over. She was very puzzled.

Finally, Mr. Craft spoke. "Haley, do you know why you're here?"

She shrugged. "No," she replied truthfully, "Mrs. Vasey said that you needed to talk with me."

Mr. Craft leaned back in his chair. "We found more oil on the slide this morning. Would you happen to know anything about it?" he inquired. His voice sounded strained.

Haley was shocked. More oil? On the slide? She was pretty sure she had done a good job of cleaning the slide. There should not have been any oil left on it. The teacher had even checked it before letting her go home. Unconsciously, she began to rub her chin.

Haley answered carefully, "No. I cleaned it up last week. There shouldn't be any oil left on the slide."

There were a few seconds of silence before Mr. Craft spoke again. His voice sounded sterner. "Haley, more oil was put on the slide this morning—a lot more oil. A girl went down the slide during one of the earlier recesses. She went down really fast, flew off the end, and landed hard. So hard, in fact, that she broke her wrist. Not only that, but she got vegetable oil all over her clothes."

The grim look had not left his face.

"We had to call her mother, who took her to the hospital to have her wrist put in a cast. Obviously, she's in tremendous pain. This squeeze bottle was found near the slide. Haley, are you trying to tell me you didn't put more oil on the slide?"

Haley was bewildered. Why would Mr. Craft think it was her? It did

not make sense. She blurted out, "NO! It wasn't me. I don't know anything about it!"

Mr. Craft shook his head. "Haley, I don't think I believe you," he said firmly.

"Why don't you believe me?" she protested. "Why would I lie? I didn't lie last time."

"I'm sorry, Haley," he said, "but I'm going to have to suspend you. I want you to wait by the receptionist while I call your mother. I'll want to talk with her before she takes you home."

Before Haley could protest further, Mr. Craft rose and guided her to the door.

She sat across from the receptionist as she had before with Red and Claudia. This time, the receptionist did not give her a kind look. Her eyes stayed focused on her computer screen.

A panicked feeling rose in Haley's throat. Suspended! Just the sound of the word caused Haley to tremble. She knew she was in very serious trouble. But she did not understand how she got there. How did the oil get on the slide again? Why did Mr. Craft not believe her?

The bell rang announcing the start of the lunch period for the fourth, fifth, and sixth graders. Haley was not hungry anymore. Instead, her stomach felt tight and jumpy.

Haley heard a sound. "Pssst."

She looked up. Red and Claudia huddled at the door. Red glanced over at the receptionist and back to Haley. She was clearly trying to see whether it was safe for her and Claudia to come in the room and sit with Haley.

Haley shrugged her shoulders. She did not know whether the receptionist would stop them or not.

Red tugged at Claudia's sleeve and they both walked in as though they were supposed to be there. Red kept stealing glances at the receptionist, but she did not look away from her computer. The girls made their way to the chairs and sat on either side of Haley.

"How'd you know I was at the principal's office?" Haley asked.

Red explained, "I didn't know. I guessed. I figured that was the most likely place you'd be. As soon as the bell rang, I went and got Claudia. Why are you here?"

In hushed tones, Haley told them about her conversation with the principal.

"Suspended!" Claudia exclaimed. The receptionist glanced at her. She lowered her voice, "You didn't put oil on the slide. We were with you before school and at recess. Red was with you in your class all morning. We'll just tell Mr. Craft that."

"I don't think he'll believe you," Haley said. Despair crept into her voice, "He's mad about the girl who got hurt, and they found another squeeze bottle just like mine. He's convinced I did it."

Red broke in, "But we know you didn't. I think you were set up by someone."

"Set up? That doesn't make sense. Who would want to do that to me?" Haley asked skeptically.

A gleam entered Red's eyes. "I have some ideas," she said with a determined voice. "But one way or another, we're gonna find out who did it."

Red and Claudia quickly left.

Haley was alone again. "I hope they find who did it, and fast," she murmured to herself.

Mrs. Bellamy looked very troubled when she arrived. Her expression did not change even after the receptionist greeted her warmly. She quickly sat next to Haley.

"I was in the middle of an important meeting when Mr. Craft called. Normally my assistant would not interrupt a meeting, but Mr. Craft left the message that it was urgent," she said. Her troubled expression changed to agitation before she continued. "We didn't talk very long, but he told me you put more oil on the slide and a girl hurt her wrist. Moreover, you're going to be suspended! Why in the world would you put more oil on the slide?"

In voice barely above a whisper, Haley said, "But Mom, I didn't do it. Mr. Craft doesn't believe me, but I didn't do it." Her voice wavered as she spoke.

Mrs. Bellamy shook her head. "But Mr. Craft said they found another one of the squeeze bottles just like you used before."

Before Haley could respond, the door to the principal's office opened. Mr. Craft appeared. "Mrs. Bellamy…"

She turned to Haley. "Wait here," she said. Her tone was firm. "We'll talk about this more after we get home."

Haley's feelings turned once more to dread.

Haley waited. It seemed like a long time had gone by and her mother was still inside the principal's office talking with Mr. Craft. She looked at the clock on the wall. She realized she had now been here almost an hour since she first arrived. The bell signaling the end to the lunch recess would ring shortly.

Suddenly, a small crowd of people entered the receptionist area. The crowd included Red, Claudia, the teacher who had escorted Haley earlier, all the members of the CATT Club, and Cage West! Red had a look of triumph on her face. Claudia looked very pleased with herself too.

The teacher told everyone to wait. He knocked briefly before disappearing inside the principal's office.

There were not enough chairs for everyone. The CATT Club stood in a small cluster as far away from Haley as they could get. They did not talk. Even loud Cynthia was silent.

Cage West stood by himself next to the receptionist's desk.

Red and Claudia plopped down on the chairs with Haley.

"What's going on?" Haley whispered.

"You'll see in just a minute," Red chortled.

Sure enough, Mrs. Bellamy came out of Mr. Craft's office in a few minutes. The teacher also came out and dismissed Cage, who had not said a word since arriving. The CATT Club was ushered into the principal's office. Mrs. Bellamy seemed far less agitated than before but still had an uncertain look on her face. She did not speak to Haley but instead stood as though she were waiting for something.

The door opened again. Mr. Craft stepped through and spoke quietly to Mrs. Bellamy. He turned to Haley.

"Haley, it seems I was wrong. I may have been too quick to assume the culprit was you. You may return to your class."

He turned again to Mrs. Bellamy and said, "And please accept my apology for disturbing you before I had all the facts."

"I'm not being suspended?" Haley asked in disbelief.

Mr. Craft gave a small smile. "No, you're not being suspended. Now, if you'll excuse me." He disappeared once more into his office where the CATT Club waited.

Haley, Red, and Claudia slowly walked back to their classes. Mrs. Bellamy had said very little to Haley, other than to convey she was not in trouble and they would talk more at home later.

"So what happened? Why am I not in trouble? Why was the CATT

Club there?" Haley asked. She still felt as though she were in a daze.

"We found who really did it. It was the CATT Club! They put vegetable oil on the slide and left a plastic squeeze bottle there so everyone would think it was you," Red said excitedly.

Claudia piped up, "Actually, it was Cage who found out."

"Cage!" Haley was surprised.

"Well, it was that boy I think likes you. You know, Cage West," Red admitted. "We went around asking everyone we could think of whether they had seen or heard anything about the oil on the slide. Cage overheard us asking. On his own, he talked with some fifth grade boys who said they saw the CATT Club near the slides in the earlier recess. So later, he hangs around near the CATT Club and overhears Cynthia bragging that she got you in trouble.

"He finds us and tells us what happened. Claudia and I find the teacher and tell him. He goes and talks with Cynthia, Andrea, and Victoria. They deny it completely. While he's talking with them, he sees Cynthia trying to hide a backpack that's sitting partially open on the bench of the lunch table. The teacher asks about the backpack. Cynthia accidentally knocks it off the bench and guess what rolls out!"

Haley did not have an idea. "What?" she asked.

"This is the great part," Red said gleefully. "A half empty bottle of vegetable oil falls out and goes rolling across the floor. The squeeze bottle was a plant. Right then, the teacher knew she was lying!"

"I'm glad we found out the truth," Claudia chimed in. "I didn't want you to get suspended."

"Wow!" Haley said. "I'm surprised Cynthia would do this to me. She must really hate me."

"In some ways, I think it's my fault," Claudia said sadly. "If you hadn't helped me, they wouldn't be so mad at you."

"That's nonsense," Haley quickly responded. "I'd still do it again, even knowing how bad the CATT Club hates me."

Claudia brightened. The girls separated at the corridor intersection. Claudia headed to her class. Red and Haley walked the rest of the way to Mrs. Vasey's classroom.

As they entered, Mrs. Vasey did not say anything, but looked pleased to see them.

Haley looked over at Cage and gave a small wave. Although it was hard to tell, Haley thought she saw a shy smile from under the long hair falling over his face.

CHAPTER 14

Kind to the CATT Club?

The last few hours of school passed without further incident. But Haley realized her goal of an uneventful week had failed. True, she had been falsely accused, but her close shave with suspension had left her shaken. When the final bell rang, she breathed a sigh of relief.

Since returning from the principal's office, Haley's perspective on the CATT Club had changed a lot. Whereas Red was easily angered by the actions of the CATT Club, Haley had usually chosen to ignore them. In some ways, she had considered them in the way she might a poisonous jellyfish. If they were right in the way, she would give them a wide berth and go around them. If they floated her way, she moved to the side to let them pass. The only time she deliberately had engaged them was when she helped Claudia. Even when the CATT Club almost hit Haley and her friends with their bicycles, she still did not get upset.

It was different now. The CATT Club, and Cynthia in particular, had tried to get Haley suspended from school. In Haley's mind, they had crossed a line. They were no longer easily ignored. They had become vicious and vindictive, almost like animals that attacked for sport.

In contrast to her usual even-keeled personality, she was seething with anger by the end of school. She decided that she hated Cynthia, Andrea, and Victoria—plain and simple. The feelings of anger and rage surprised her. In some ways, her fury felt really good. Yet at the same time, it also scared her too because it was as though control of her emotions had been wrestled away from her. In any case, she was sure whatever suspension the members of the CATT Club received, it would not be long enough.

When Haley arrived home, she was surprised at her mother's greeting. Usually, Mrs. Bellamy would be busy working at the family room table on her accounting. Her typical greeting would be to glance up at Haley and ask a quick, "How was your day, honey," before returning to her work.

Today there was no evidence of accounting paperwork downstairs at all. Plus, Mrs. Bellamy had both a snack and hot cider waiting for her. Most astounding was her mother's choice of foods for Haley's snack. On her plate were slices of pepperoni, cheese, and, most surprising, cheese puffs!

Haley decided not to question her mother about the snack in case she might change her mind to healthier foods. They said very little while Haley ate. Mostly, Haley's mind was preoccupied with thoughts of the CATT Club and how mad she was at them.

After the snack, Haley sat on the sofa in the living room. Einstein curled into a ball on her lap. She clutched the mug of steaming apple cider that had a little cinnamon stick poking out the top. Mrs. Bellamy lounged on the sofa next to her, also holding a mug of apple cider.

After a long while, Mrs. Bellamy finally said, "It's been quite a day, hasn't it."

Haley agreed with a brief, "Yep."

Mrs. Bellamy waited a few more seconds. When Haley did not say anything further, she broke the silence again. "Haley, even though I had to leave work early, I'm glad it wasn't you who put the oil on the slide this time."

"You still thought I did it at first," Haley responded, with a touch of irritation in her voice.

Mrs. Bellamy nodded. "At first," she admitted. "But, I was going on the basis of what Mr. Craft told me over the telephone. Remember, they found another squeeze bottle by the slide."

Haley did not say anything. She slowly stirred her cider with the cinnamon stick and waited.

"Fortunately," Mrs. Bellamy continued, "they found the kids who really did it." She paused for a moment. "I still don't understand why they would want to make it seem like you did it. Who were those girls? Why were they trying to get you in trouble?"

"That was Cynthia, Andrea, and Victoria from the CATT Club. I told you about them before. They're the ones who kept pushing Claudia around," she said.

Her voice grew louder. "I hate them," she said with raw emotion. "I hate them more than I've hated anything before. I'm glad they're suspended. I hope they're suspended forever!"

She was shocked at the venom in her own voice. It was almost as though the words were being spoken by someone else, not Haley.

From the look on her mother's face, she was very surprised too. "Haley, I've never heard you talk like this before. Are you—"

Haley did not let her finish her sentence. "Yeah, I'm sure. They're mean to everyone! They pushed Claudia around. They almost hit us with their bikes. They put oil on the slide to get me in trouble. Every time I think about it, I hate them more and more."

Mrs. Bellamy shook her head. "Hating them isn't the answer. Hating will make you do things you wouldn't do otherwise. You might even do something that you would regret later," she said.

Haley was not convinced. She said, "Right now it feels pretty good." She saw her mother giving her one of those you-are-not-listening-to-me looks. She rolled her eyes, "Okay," she sighed, "what do *you* think I should be doing?"

"Well," said Mrs. Bellamy carefully, "you could try love."

"Love!" Haley sputtered.

"Okay," said Mrs. Bellamy, retreating slightly. "Let's call it another name. How about kindness?"

Haley stared at her.

"Haven't you heard the expression *Love your enemy*?"[5] she asked.

Haley shook her head.

Mrs. Bellamy persisted, "You don't remember it from Sunday school?"

Haley shook her head again.

Now it was Mrs. Bellamy's turn to sigh. "What's the point of going if you're not learning anything? From now on, I'm going to start asking you about what you learned there."

She motioned with her mug. "The idea is kindness can be very powerful. How do you think Cynthia would react if you did something nice for her, or were kind to her?"

Haley considered the question. "I don't know," was her response.

"Wouldn't she be surprised?" Mrs. Bellamy asked. She pressed further. "I don't know, but maybe she's mean to other people because she doesn't get enough love and kindness at home. Maybe she's thirsting for both."

"I didn't really think about it," Haley admitted.

Her mother continued, "It's really all part of how we want to be treated, and how we see others—even people who are mean to us. Just as

5. Luke 6:35

we don't gloat over the misfortune of others,[6] we shouldn't treat them poorly. Even if they rebuff our kindness, we shouldn't change ourselves and become like them."

Listening to her mother, Haley could feel her anger at Cynthia starting to ease. But it certainly was not gone. "I don't think I can be nice to Cynthia right now. I'm still mad. How can I be kind to her when I'm feeling this way?"

"You're right. She did a terrible thing and got you in trouble," Mrs. Bellamy agreed. "I don't think you'll be able to try doing something until you can get rid of your anger. It sounds like the first thing you should try is to forgive Cynthia."

"Forgive her?" Haley asked. "Why?"

"Because, if nothing else, it'll be good for you, even if Cynthia doesn't respond. It'll help you to let go of your anger. Give it a try," Mrs. Bellamy suggested. "You don't have to say it out loud if you don't want to. Try telling it to yourself."

Haley closed her eyes and breathed deeply. She could smell the cinnamon and apple from the cider. Thoughts of Cynthia and the CATT Club flooded her head. Even if forgiving Cynthia was good for her, it was still going to be hard to do. Haley wasn't sure she could do it. She was pretty sure saying the words wouldn't help very much if she didn't try to mean it.

The back of her neck felt stiff. She wondered if that was because of her anger. She tried lowering her shoulders and relaxing her arms. Slowly, her mind pushed away everything except Cynthia's face. "I forgive you, Cynthia," she said silently to herself.

A cool wave seemed to wash through her body, taking much of her rage with it. Her anger was not gone, but it was far less. She tried again.

6. Proverbs 24:17

"I forgive you," she repeated silently.

Another wave washed through her, lowering her frustration further. But still some remained. She opened her eyes to find her mother looking at her carefully.

"Well?" asked Mrs. Bellamy.

"In my mind, I told her that I forgave her," Haley said. "I feel much better. I'm not nearly as mad. But I don't feel like it's completely gone. Shouldn't it be?"

Mrs. Bellamy put her arm around Haley and gave her a hug. "You'd think so," she said, "but it doesn't work like that. When we forgive, it doesn't mean that we forget. It's hard to let go when someone was really bad to us. We can get mad again, even though we already forgave the person. What that means is that you sometimes need to forgive someone more than once. There's a place in the bible, the book of Matthew I think, where someone asked Jesus whether you should forgive someone seven times. His response was not seven times, but seventy times seven.[7]

"There really isn't an exact number. The point is that we may need to extend forgiveness many times to keep ourselves from going backwards in our relationship with that person. You'll have to see how you feel about Cynthia and the other girls. You might find you need to forgive them again. Think about yourself. If you feel like you're getting mad again and it's starting to control you, it's probably a good time to forgive her again. I wish it were as easy as saying it once, but it's not."

Haley let the words sink in. She felt better at the moment, but she wondered how she would feel when she saw Cynthia and the CATT Club at school again.

Haley made it through the rest of the week without incident. Despite

7. Matthew 18:22

her attempts at forgiveness, Haley still hoped the CATT Club would not return until the next week just to allow more time to go by. However, as it turned out, the CATT Club's suspension lasted only a day and a half, which meant they were back in school on Friday.

She saw Victoria and Andrea in the hallway, but they seemed to keep their distance from her. At recess, the CATT Club could be seen in a small cluster off to the side of the school yard. They kept to themselves, although they looked in Haley's direction several times. Red commented to Haley that they were the quietest and nicest she could remember. Apparently, the suspension had taken away much of their confidence and bravado. Haley, Red, and Claudia kept their distance to avoid any possibility of contact.

The weekend started with a cold snap unlike anything Ann Arbor had seen in decades. It was only the third week in November and the temperatures plunged close to zero, although there was not any snow. The slight breeze made it feel colder still. Even the bare tree branches trembled from the cold. The temperature was the main topic on every television channel Haley watched.

On Sunday, Haley did not think her family would go to church given the brisk cold. But she was wrong. Her mother pointed out it was not any colder than in January, and, with no snow, it was not like they needed to shovel the driveway before they could go anywhere. Haley was glad her mother made the family go because she saw Claudia again at her Sunday school class.

"Do you want to come over to my house this afternoon?" Claudia asked. "My grandmother wants to make some decorations for Thanksgiving."

"Sure," Haley replied. "That'll be a whole lot better than sitting home and watching television with my dad and my brother. All they want to watch is football. Who wants to see people knocking each other over trying to get a little ball? I don't get it."

Claudia giggled. "It does seem like a dumb game. We'll definitely have more fun than that. Maybe Red can come too."

"I'll call her when I get home," Haley said. She had an idea. "We could even walk to the pond near your house and see how much is frozen."

They were interrupted by the start of the class. Claudia leaned across to Haley and whispered, "We never get to finish our conversation before class starts. We can talk more after church."

Red met Haley at her house before they headed together to Claudia's. It was too cold to ride bicycles. They bundled themselves in thick parkas, wool mittens, and insulated boots. The heavy clothes made them waddle stiffly.

They could see the frost from their breath as they exhaled.

"I can barely move," Red grumbled loudly. "I feel like I'm a walking sausage."

Haley laughed at Red's comment. She could see her breath making little puffs that looked like tiny clouds. "Are you a link sausage or a patty sausage?" she joked.

Red frowned at her.

Haley leaned over and bumped Red with her shoulder. "Actually, I think we look more like penguins. You know how they waddle from side to side?"

"Hey, don't bump," Red complained. "If I fall over, I won't be able to get back up."

"Don't worry," Haley chided, "I'll just roll you the rest of the way. I guess that makes you more of a link sausage. If you were a penguin, you'd be able to get up by yourself."

Red used a mitten to push her glasses farther onto her nose.

Haley leaned over to bump Red with her shoulder again. She missed. Red had stopped. Haley almost tumbled over herself, but fortunately she bumped against a chain link fence and gained her balance.

"Wow. Look at that!" Red exclaimed. She pointed with her mitten.

Haley turned to see Red pointing at the school building.

They were at the school fence. Red pointed at the workers on the roof of the school. Huge clouds of steam billowed all around them. It looked like they were spraying hot water on the roof with a high-pressure hose.

"What do you think they're doing?" Red asked.

"I don't know," Haley replied. "I thought they'd be done with their work by now. Maybe they're doing a final cleaning."

"It almost looks like smoke from a fire," Red observed.

"It's steam from the water. They must be using hot water so it doesn't freeze while they're spraying the roof," Haley explained.

They watched for a few more minutes before continuing on their way.

Claudia was waiting for them when they arrived. They quickly shed their parkas, mittens, and boots. After the frosty air outside, Claudia's house felt inviting and cozy. The girls gathered around the dining table. There were construction paper, glue, scissors, pens, and various feathers, pine cones, and other things already on the table.

"I think it's too cold to go to the pond," Haley said.

"I think it's too cold, period," Red stated firmly.

Claudia grinned. "We can stay inside. My grandmother has plenty of Thanksgiving decoration stuff we can work on. If we get tired of that, we can do something else."

Haley picked up a pine cone and looked at it. She pulled out her

magnifying glass and peered in the crevasses.

Red piped up. "Did you see Cynthia and the rest of the CATT Club on Friday? They didn't bother anybody. It's about time they got into trouble."

"Do you think they learned their lesson?" Claudia wondered out loud.

Red snorted. "I don't think so. They'll lay low for a while, but then they'll be back to their old ways. They're just mean—plain and simple," she said resolutely. "The best thing to do is stay as far away from them as you can get."

Haley looked up from her pine cone. "My mom says I should try and be kind to them," she said.

"What!" Red sputtered. "Your mom is nuts. They almost got you suspended forever."

"I know," Haley acknowledged. "I was really mad at them. I was so mad that I didn't even feel like my normal self."

Haley told them about her conversation with her mother. Claudia was open to the idea that Haley could try to find some way to show kindness to Cynthia. "It couldn't hurt to try once," she said.

"That'd be like trying to feed a bear," Red said seriously. "It might take food from your hand or it might just eat your hand."

It was clear Red and Claudia disagreed whether Haley should follow her mother's advice. Haley felt confused. Before, she thought she might try it, but now she was not sure. She decided to figure it out later. While her friends continued to banter back and forth, Haley sighed and turned her attention back to her pine cone.

∾ CHAPTER 15 ∾

The Broken Glass Experiment

During the night, the cold snap broke and the temperatures started to rise. By the time Haley arrived at school Monday morning, the temperatures had risen into the mid-thirties. It still felt cold to Haley, but at least she did not need to wear her parka. She still wore the insulated boots but was able to make do with her normal winter coat.

Even before she tried to go inside the school building, she was intercepted by Red and Claudia. They rushed to her and pulled her next to the building. Haley could see Red had that same look of triumph she had the week before when she strode into the principal's office with the CATT Club in tow. In contrast to Red, Claudia's face wore a slight frown.

"Did you hear?" Red asked excitedly. She was bouncing around so much that she needed to keep one hand on her glasses to keep them from falling off her face.

"Hear what?" Haley had no idea what Red was talking about.

"She just got here. How would she know?" Claudia said in an exasperated voice. "We didn't find out until we got here too."

Haley was thoroughly mystified. "I have no idea what you're talking about," she said.

"Cynthia and the CATT Club," Red announced as though Haley should have figured it out by now. "They're in big trouble—even bigger trouble than last week. Do you know what they did?"

Red did not give Haley a chance to guess before she continued, "They broke a bunch of windows on the other side of the building. I heard all the windows on the entire side were smashed. The whole school's talking about it."

Haley was shocked. The CATT Club broke school windows? That did not make sense to her, especially after they were suspended last week. The CATT Club might be mean, but they were not dumb.

Claudia was still frowning. "We don't have to be happy about it," she pointed out to Red. "Don't you remember what we talked about yesterday? Haley said her mom told her it's not right to be happy when someone else is in trouble."

"Anyone else and I might agree with you," said Red. "But we're talking about the same girls who set up Haley."

"Let's not talk about that now," Haley suggested. "Let's go see the windows."

Red was still bouncing. "Right," she agreed.

The girls walked around the building until they got to the side with the broken windows. It was the side that faced the playground. It was easy to figure out where the broken windows were because there was a crowd of kids and teachers watching the unfolding situation.

The girls joined the crowd. Sure enough, just as Red had said, there were a number of windows broken along the side of the building. One teacher roamed back and forth in front of the windows, brushing back children who tried to venture too close.

Off to the side, Haley could see the CATT Club huddled together. Standing next to them was Mr. Craft, the janitor, and another teacher.

Mr. Craft seemed to be in conversation with the other adults. He gestured several times and pointed to the broken windows.

Haley edged closer to the windows. Red and Claudia stayed with her as she nudged her way past other children.

From her vantage point, Haley could clearly see the damage. The windows were set high on the wall. The bottom edge of the windows was about at the same height as the top of the teacher's head. Six windows were clearly broken. Several pieces had fallen and smashed upon the ground. Sunlight glinted off the tiny shards.

Haley stared at the windows along the side. She noticed some of the windows were more broken than others. Three windows barely had any glass remaining. Two windows had large jagged pieces still in the window frame. One window had a small piece missing but also had a number of cracks. She noticed two other windows had a few cracks but had not broken. She absentmindedly began to rub her chin.

Slowly, an idea began to form in her mind. Then it hit her.

She moved quickly to the side and walked away from the crowd. Red and Claudia saw her go and followed. They looked at each other and shrugged.

"She's doing it again," Claudia whispered to Red. "She's got something on her mind. What could she be thinking about?"

Red said, "We watch. We follow."

The girls entered the school through the side door. The hallway was empty. It seemed everyone had gone outside to see the damage.

The hallway was still cold, although not as cold as the outside air. Haley remembered the school kept the furnaces off over the weekends to save money. It made her more convinced that she might be right.

Haley found the classrooms that faced the playground. She looked inside each one until she found one that had broken windows. Fortunately, it was empty. Apparently, the teacher was outside along with everyone else.

Haley made her way to the side of the classroom that bordered the windows, scanning the entire room as she went. There were no signs of rocks, sticks, or anything else that might have been thrown through the window.

The windows were high along the wall. Two of the windows had large chunks of glass missing. Another had large, jagged pieces remaining.

She looked on the floor. Pieces of the window had fallen inside the classroom. There were pieces of glass scattered all over the floor. Haley crouched. She could see glass splinters resting in what looked like small puddles of water. She rose again.

Farther along the wall was a reading couch. It was a dark green with soft overstuffed cushions. Haley studied the couch until she saw what she had hoped to find. A large piece of glass was on one cushion. It had landed without breaking further, although it still had sharp, jagged edges.

She pulled out her magnifying glass and scanned the shard. Through the magnifying glass, she saw spots where water had dried. It confirmed what she suspected. She turned to Red and Claudia, who had been patiently observing her. "The CATT Club didn't break these windows," she stated.

Red looked at her skeptically. "Are you kidding? The principal has Cynthia and her gang already. Of course they did it. Mr. Craft wouldn't grab them unless he was sure."

"He was sure when I almost got suspended," Haley retorted. "But you proved that it wasn't me."

Red adjusted her glasses. "He wouldn't make the same mistake again. After you, I'm sure he's being extra careful to make sure he has the right person. Why do you think it wasn't them?"

She showed them the shard and explained how she thought the window broke. "I'm sure I'm right. And, I bet I can prove it," Haley said.

Red still seemed skeptical, but Claudia nodded in agreement. "I think she's right," she said. "It probably wasn't Cynthia."

Red snorted. "Even if the CATT Club didn't break the windows, why in the world would you want to help them? They set you up and almost got you suspended."

"True," Haley agreed, "but it's not right if they're being accused when they didn't do it. I didn't like it when I was falsely accused. I'm sure they're not any different. Besides, maybe this is the opportunity to do something nice for Cynthia like my mom suggested."

Claudia voiced her support. "I agree with Haley. We've got nothing to lose."

Red sighed, "Out-voted again. Okay, I'm with you. What do you want to do, Haley?"

Haley explained her plan. The girls headed out of the classroom and back down the hallway. The excitement outside must have finished, because children and teachers started to fill the hall.

The girls turned the corner into the corridor and almost bumped into Mrs. Vasey.

"Where are you girls going?" she asked. "The excitement outside is over. Everyone needs to go to their classrooms."

"Mrs. Vasey, is Mr. Craft still outside?" Haley inquired.

"No, he's gone back to his office," Mrs. Vasey replied. "Why are you looking for him?"

Haley explained the reasons she did not think Cynthia, Andrea, and Victoria had anything to do with the broken windows.

Mrs. Vasey listened carefully. As Haley finished, she raised an eyebrow.

"It's almost time for music class," she said. "I'll take the class to Mrs. Heppie's room for music, then I'll take you to Mr. Craft's office. You can explain it to him and see what he thinks."

She turned to Red and Claudia. "Claudia, please go back to your classroom. Red, you'll need to stay in Mrs. Heppie's along with the rest of the class."

The girls and Mrs. Vasey entered the receptionist area of the principal's office. Cynthia, Andrea, and Victoria were sitting in a neat row. They did not look happy at all. In fact, their heads were down. Andrea wiped something from her eyes. Haley was certain it was tears. She also heard Victoria sniffing. Cynthia simply stared at the floor.

Haley waited by the receptionist while Mrs. Vasey slipped into Mr. Craft's office. None of the members of the CATT Club looked in their direction.

After a few minutes, Mrs. Vasey reappeared and motioned for Haley to come inside. Haley entered and sat in the same chair as before, only this time Mrs. Vasey sat next to her. Mr. Craft was pacing behind his desk.

He stopped and looked at Haley. "Mrs. Vasey tells me that you don't think Cynthia, Andrea, and Victoria had anything to do with the broken windows," he said.

Haley felt her courage starting to wane. It was one thing to tell Red and Claudia her theory. It was another to tell the principal of the school. She swallowed hard.

"Yes sir," Haley said politely.

"You know that one of the teachers who lives across the street from the school saw the girls next to the school building on Sunday morning?" he asked.

Haley had not known that. She was suddenly afraid. What if she was wrong and the CATT Club *had* broken the windows?

"Did they say what they were doing there?" Haley inquired.

Mr. Craft breathed in deeply and stretched his neck. He looked tense. "They said they were on their way to Victoria's house and just taking a shortcut across the school. I asked them whether they saw any broken windows then, but they all said no."

Haley reasoned it was possible they were telling the truth. "What time did the teacher see them?" she asked.

Mr. Craft looked at her quizzically, "It was early, about 9:00 a.m. Why do you ask?"

She did not immediately answer. Instead she asked another question. "What time did the maintenance crew start their work on the roof?"

The look on his face made it clear that he did not know where Haley's questions were going. "The workers started around 11:00 a.m. or so. Why are you asking about them? What do they have to do with anything?"

Haley was relieved. The girls had passed the school well before the work crew arrived. At last she explained, "I'm certain they didn't break the windows. There's broken glass both inside the classrooms and outside on the pavement. The windows are higher than the heads of any of the girls. If they threw something at the window, all of the glass would have fallen inside the building, but it didn't. Also, some of the windows had only cracks. Besides, I went inside one of the classrooms and didn't see a rock or anything that might have been thrown. I'm convinced they couldn't have broken the windows."

Haley clearly had Mr. Craft's attention. "So who do you think broke the windows?" he asked cautiously.

"I think the workers did. Not on purpose, of course. Since they were working on the roof, they probably didn't even realize they had broken any windows," she said.

Mr. Craft looked attentive. "I don't follow you. How could they have broken the windows?" he asked.

Haley began to feel more confident. She said, "The windows in the school are really old. They're the same windows from when the school was built, so the glass has to be over 50 years old. The glass is really thin too.

"This weekend was super cold. I saw the workers spraying hot water on the roof on Sunday when Red and I were on our way to Claudia's house. I think the hot water dripped over the side of the roof and down onto the cold windows. The school furnace is off on weekends. The temperature inside the room and outside was probably the same, so the glass in the windows had to have been close to zero degrees. When the warm water touched the glass, it created a high temperature gradient. Glass has low conductivity. It created thermal shock and cracked the glass. I even found some small puddles of water in the classroom and dried water spots on a piece of glass. I think all the water outside the classroom must have evaporated," she concluded.

Mr. Craft looked at Haley. She was not sure whether his look suggested she was brilliant, or insane.

He slowly asked, "So why were the windows broken only on the one side?"

Haley had anticipated his question. "Because all the other sides of the building have eaves that extend out. That side is the only one without eaves."

The room fell silent. Haley glanced at Mrs. Vasey, who was still sitting next to her. Mrs. Vasey gave her a wink.

Mr. Craft ran his hand through his grey hair. "Haley, I'm impressed with your knowledge and ideas. Your explanation sounds plausible, although I'm not entirely convinced about warm water causing the glass to break. I don't know, it just sounds pretty unlikely."

Haley was taken aback. She had expected him to accept her explanation. She was not sure what to say.

"You don't want to get the wrong person," she pleaded. "I know what it's like to be accused of something you didn't do. I'm not Cynthia's friend, but I don't want to see anyone get punished if they're innocent."

Mr. Craft looked slightly embarrassed.

A soft voice said, "Uh, Mr. Craft." It was Mrs. Vasey. Haley glanced in her direction.

The principal switched his gaze from Haley to her.

She leaned forward. "Couldn't we do an experiment to see if warm water could cause the glass to break?" she inquired.

He looked doubtful. "An experiment?"

Right then, Haley knew exactly how she could prove it. "Yes," she said eagerly, "an experiment!"

She explained her idea to them. Mrs. Vasey beamed. Mr. Craft nodded his head.

"Okay Haley. If you can show me the glass can break, you'll have removed the last reservation I have about your explanation," he said. "Until then, I won't take any actions with Cynthia, Andrea, or Victoria."

Haley was relieved. She felt confident her experiment would work.

Mrs. Vasey went with Haley back to the classroom with the broken windows. The room was still empty. The children who would normally be in the room were in the library until the janitor could clean up the glass and tape plastic sheeting over the broken windows.

Haley found the large piece of glass on the sofa where she left it. Mrs.

Vasey carried the shard to the teacher's lounge. The lounge had a refrigerator and freezer. Mrs. Vasey took a plate from the lounge kitchen cabinet. Haley placed the piece of glass on the plate and put it in the freezer. The freezer had both a dial and a separate temperature gauge. The gauge read twenty five degrees. Haley turned the temperature dial to its coldest setting.

"The lowest setting should get the glass close to zero degrees, about the same temperature as yesterday," she explained. "All we need to do is wait a couple of hours so the glass is as cold as possible."

While they were in the lounge, they saw the janitor. Mrs. Vasey asked him to contact the maintenance company and find out the water temperature of their sprayer.

Mrs. Vasey walked with Haley to the music classroom. "We'll need to wait until the lunch recess before we try the experiment," she said.

Haley was excited. She wanted to try the experiment now, but knew she had to wait. She was certain she was right, but she, of all people, knew experiments did not always work as planned. She desperately wanted this experiment to work. It seemed like the clock in the classroom moved more slowly than normal.

Finally, it was time. The bell rang to signal the beginning of lunch. Haley and Red ran ahead swiftly through the hallway to the teachers' lounge. Mrs. Vasey followed. They found Claudia in the corridor along the way and told her the plan.

In the teacher's lounge, Haley saw Mr. Craft and the janitor waiting for them.

"The janitor called the maintenance company," he explained. "Their sprayer heated the water to 95 degrees to keep it from freezing while they were working."

He held out something in his hand. "Here's a thermometer you can

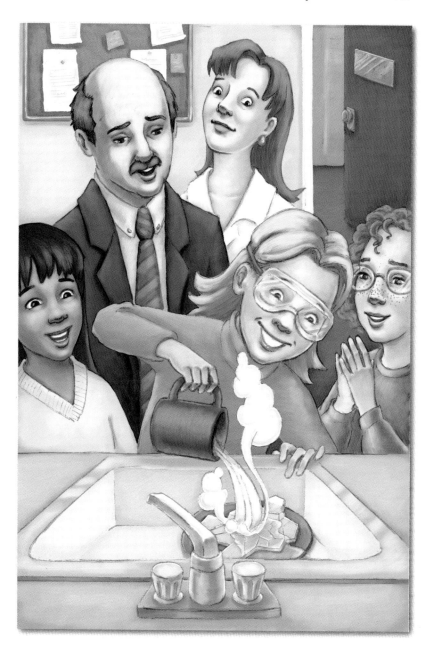

use to measure the water temperature. I borrowed it from the school nurse."

Haley took the thermometer. She ran the water at the sink until the thermometer registered a consistent 95 degrees. She filled a mug with water.

Next, she went to the freezer and looked inside. The gauge now read minus five degrees. It was close enough for the experiment.

This was the moment of truth. Either Haley's theory would be proved or disproved. If it worked, all suspicions of the CATT Club would be lifted. If it didn't work, it was likely the CATT Club would be suspended, or worse.

Haley breathed deeply. She looked over at Red and Claudia. They both gave her a thumbs-up. She put on a pair of safety goggles the janitor gave her. Haley glanced at Mrs. Vasey. She simply nodded.

Haley said a quick silent prayer: *God, please make this work.*

With that, she pulled the plate from the freezer and quickly placed it in the sink. Everyone crowded around her. She grabbed the mug of warm water and poured it on the piece of glass.

The effect was immediate. As soon as the water touched the piece of glass, it cracked and broke. A loud *Snap* could be heard.

Haley felt her heart leap. It worked! Just like she had predicted.

Claudia and Mrs. Vasey clapped. Red yelled a loud, "Yeah!"

Mr. Craft turned to Haley. His lips were pursed and his head bobbed up and down in agreement. "Haley," he said, "you've convinced me."

∽ CHAPTER 16 ∽

The Problem With Garbage

Haley was hunched over her school desk, with her face close to her paper. The pencil in her hand hovered over the paper. The bell rang, interrupting her concentration. The writing assignment the class received after lunch proved to be much harder than she imagined. Sighing, she straightened and looked down at her paper. There were only a few words scrawled on it. Not enough to consider the assignment complete. Writing was not her favorite subject anyway. It was a distant fourth after science, math, and reading.

She became aware that the rest of the class had packed their backpacks and were leaving. The only people lingering were Red and Mrs. Vasey.

Haley handed her paper to Mrs. Vasey and said apologetically, "I didn't get very far on the assignment."

Taking the paper, Mrs. Vasey did not even look at it before replying, "That's okay, Haley. It's been a busy day. I think your accomplishments with the experiment and helping those girls are more important for now. We'll work together on the writing assignment later in the week."

When Haley and Red emerged from their classroom, Claudia was already waiting in the hall. The girls headed for the front of the school.

"I'm glad the day's over," said Claudia. "It's just too much excitement for me!"

"Not for me," Red chimed in. "It'd be too boring otherwise. That's why I hang around Haley. I know with her, excitement is always just around the corner."

"Gee Red, thanks," Haley said sarcastically. She continued in a weary tone of voice. "I wouldn't mind a few days of boredom where absolutely nothing exciting happened."

It was true. What Haley wanted most was to get through an entire week without blowing anything up, setting something on fire, spraying water everywhere, breaking windows, cleaning oily slides, or nearly getting suspended. Haley wondered if she should force herself to sit on the sofa at home next to J.R. and watch football the rest of the week. It might be torture, but at least it would be boring torture.

A high, gray, overcast sky greeted the girls as they emerged from the school. It gave them the feeling of late fall, with the promise of Thanksgiving in another week and the expectation that snow would soon be falling. The girls walked slowly, chatting.

Haley had not seen them earlier, but the CATT Club was coming directly toward them on an intercept course. She stiffened and nudged Red and Claudia. Their conversation trailed off.

Cynthia was in the lead, as usual, with Victoria and Andrea close behind her. The CATT Club stopped directly in front of them. The girls were forced to stop as well.

The two groups of girls eyed each other silently. Haley could feel that Red was gearing up for a confrontation. She saw all the signs—her stance and the way she pushed her glasses firmly on her nose. Haley glimpsed Claudia's face. It had a clear look of worry, but she stayed next to Haley.

Haley looked directly at Cynthia. Her dark eyes had a stern look but were not as mean as Haley remembered. However, her face was still set in a scowl. She looked very uncomfortable.

"I want to say something to you, Haley," Cynthia growled. She took a step closer.

Haley wanted to take a step back, but she held her ground.

"Thanks," Cynthia said. She jammed her hands in her pockets and looked even more uncomfortable. "If it wasn't for you, I'd be expelled."

Andrea and Victoria chimed in from behind Cynthia, "Yeah. Thanks you guys."

Haley was stunned. The CATT Club was expressing gratitude? She had not expected any appreciation for helping. She had expected the CATT Club would simply avoid everyone, including herself.

"Uh, sure," Haley said haltingly. "Glad we were able to help."

Cynthia shifted back and forth, still looking uncomfortable. "Mr. Craft explained how you proved it wasn't us who broke the windows. I still don't understand why you stuck your neck out for us. Why would you help?"

Haley looked at Cynthia. "I don't want to see anyone get in trouble—especially if they didn't do it. I know what it's like to be falsely accused," she said.

Cynthia turned red with embarrassment.

"And," Haley continued, "I wanted to do something nice for you."

Cynthia turned even redder. Her eyes narrowed, then widened. It was several seconds before she responded.

"Well, thanks again," she grumbled, "It was nice that you helped. But, this doesn't mean we're automatically friends."

The CATT Club turned and left. As Haley watched them go, she wondered whether her act of kindness would truly affect them or be short-lived, with them returning to their menacing ways.

When Haley arrived home, her mother was in her usual spot at the family room table. Accounting papers were spread around. Einstein was lying at her feet. He lifted his head and wagged his tail when Haley came in, but did not get up.

Mrs. Bellamy rose from her chair and gave Haley a warm hug. Haley was surprised. This was the second time in the last week that her mother had changed her welcome-home pattern.

"I'm so proud of you, Haley," said Mrs. Bellamy warmly. "Mr. Craft called me and told me what you did today at school. I also got a call from your teacher Mrs. Vasey. It's amazing you figured everything out. You definitely have Bellamy science genes. Tell me more about it."

Mrs. Bellamy pushed her papers aside and had Haley sit at the table. She sat next to Haley and listened carefully while Haley recounted the events of the day. Much to Haley's surprise, her mother seemed genuinely interested in the whole story, even when Haley went into detail about her thermal shock theory and the experiment.

When Haley finished, Mrs. Bellamy leaned back in her chair. "How do you feel about Cynthia and her friends now?" she asked.

Haley scratched Einstein under the chin and thought about her mother's question. "At first, I wasn't convinced that forgiving them would work. It seemed like I had to tell myself lots of times that I forgave them. But especially when I had the chance to help, it made it much easier to try.

"I don't hate them anymore if that's what you're asking. I don't know if they'll be different or not, but I feel like I made the effort and did what I could. I guess overall I feel pretty good."

Mrs. Bellamy nodded. She leaned over and gave Haley another hug. Einstein licked her chin. "Haley, I love you very much, and I'm proud of you. I think we should celebrate. Why don't you invite Red and Claudia over for an early dinner and we can have any dinner you want. What do you think about that?"

"Cool! Any dinner I want?" she asked. Haley was ecstatic.

Mrs. Bellamy nodded.

"Pizza!" Haley shouted, "But I don't want raisins and pickles like Aunt Gabby. I just want pepperoni, sausage, and olives."

"Pizza it is." Mrs. Bellamy laughed. "And we'll hold the pickles and raisins."

Red and Claudia arrived later. "I love pizza!" Red exclaimed when she found out about dinner. "Can we eat now?"

Claudia rolled her eyes. "Red, it's not polite to demand food. We're Haley's guests."

"Maybe so," Red agreed, "but my stomach is getting hungry and I—"

Haley and Claudia finished her sentence in unison. "Get crabby when you get hungry. We know," they chorused.

"My dad and J.R. are getting the pizza. They're not back yet, but it should only be a few more minutes," Haley explained.

Mrs. Bellamy interrupted the girls. "Haley, while we're waiting for the pizza, would you mind taking the garbage out to the street. Tomorrow is garbage day."

Haley protested, "But it's J.R.'s turn. Besides, I have guests."

"I know, but J.R. isn't here right now, and if we don't get it out we'll likely forget it. Please just do it," Mrs. Bellamy said.

"I always have to make up for J.R.'s slack," she grumbled, but moved toward the door anyway.

Red and Claudia followed Haley into the garage. Haley tripped over J.R.'s skateboard, which was in the middle of the floor again.

"You guys have a lot of stuff," observed Claudia as they made their way past the bicycles, boxes, and shelves.

"More like a lot of junk," Haley scoffed.

She reached the garbage can and gave it a tug. It did not move. The can was much heavier this time. She would need help.

"Can you guys help me?" Haley asked.

The girls came forward and tried to help, but the can was very heavy and awkward. After pushing on it several times, the girls stopped.

"This thing is really heavy," Red puffed.

"Isn't there anything you can use? Maybe something with wheels," Claudia panted.

They were right, Haley decided. It was time to figure out a better way to get the garbage to the street. After all, she was a scientist and inventor—and a good one. She proved that to herself when she figured out the broken windows.

She scanned the garage. There had to be something they could use. Haley spied J.R.'s skateboard.

"I've got an idea," she exclaimed.

She fetched J.R.'s skateboard and placed it next to the garbage can. She had Red and Claudia pull back on the top of the can, making it tilt. She pushed the skateboard under the tipped can and eased it back until the garbage can was balanced on the skateboard.

"See," she said, steadying the can with both hands and rolling it forward slightly. "Now I can move it myself."

Red and Claudia stood back while Haley rolled it to the edge of the garage. Claudia looked down at the steep angle of the driveway. "Are you sure this is a good idea?" she asked.

Haley pushed the can over the edge. It seemed to want to pull Haley down the driveway. She could barely keep her grip on it. "Sure," she said through gritted teeth.

But the weight of the can on the skateboard was too much for Haley.

It slipped out of her grasp and started to careen down the driveway. Haley gasped.

At the same time, the car with Mr. Bellamy and J.R. appeared, and Mr. Bellamy started to pull into the driveway. Haley watched in horror as the scene unfolded in front of her, seemingly in slow motion.

Her father slammed on the brakes, but the can was headed straight at the car. The garbage can hit the front corner of car. It bounced off wildly and fell over with a loud *bang*. Trash spewed all over as the can hit the ground and rolled to the edge of the street. J.R.'s skateboard skewed sideways and into the tire. The car wheel climbed on top the skateboard, and with a sharp *crack*, the skateboard snapped in two. The car finally halted.

At first, no one moved. Her father was frozen with disbelief. Red and Claudia gaped. J.R. looked thoroughly confused. Haley dared not move.

Slowly, J.R. and Mr. Bellamy got out of the car. Mr. Bellamy walked around the front and surveyed the scene. The front headlamp was broken and there was a large dent in the car. Trash was strewn over the driveway and sidewalk. Mr. Bellamy had the same puzzled look on his face as he had after Haley had used the toilet plunger in the bathroom sink.

J.R. leaned down next to the wheel of the car. He stood again holding the two pieces of his skateboard, one in each hand. "My skateboard," he whimpered.

Haley turned to her friends. Claudia's face was set in an expression of disbelief. Red's eyes sparkled as she adjusted her glasses. Red nudged Claudia, almost causing her to lose her balance.

"Like I told you before," Red laughed. "Welcome to the world of Haley. It's full of surprises and always exciting!"

∽ *The End* ∽

BOOKS AND DOLLS WITH A PURPOSE

www.AmyElise.com

The inspiration for *Amy Elise, Books & Dolls with a Purpose,* came from my own children. Despite all the advances made by women over the past 100 years, we still face significant challenges in our efforts to raise our daughters. Girls are asked to grow up far too fast and are confronted with a barrage of messages devoid of moral principles, which value physical appearance more than intelligence, talent, and relationships.

The fact remains as mothers we are simply trying to help our girls grow and mature and to develop a foundation of moral values that will sustain them regardless of whether they sail through life or confront difficult challenges. We believe the values that our company encourages mirror the values girls and their mothers feel are important to navigate life. Through the lens of fun and humor, our books and products focus on the basic values of kindness, generosity, courage, hope, and faith.

At Amy Elise, girls are portrayed as gifted and intelligent, and as leaders. Each girl has unique skills, abilities, and perspectives that we should all celebrate. Relationships between girls and their parents are portrayed as positive and strong, while acknowledging that conflicts and challenges do occur. Without being prescriptive, we look at faith from the girls' point of view and work to encourage them to further explore and develop their faith with the guidance and support of their parents.

In our effort to live the same values as our customers, a portion of every sale is donated to a select group of charities that meet efficient business standards and whose mission supports girls, children, or families.

Come and join us. Together, let's celebrate our daughters, give them a strong foundation, and inspire them to live their lives with purpose.

Kristin H. Wisegarver, CEO